Sherlock Holmes – A Study in Illustrations

A Collection of Early Illustrations from various publications

Volume 1

Let's face it, it's mainly Sidney Paget in this volume

Michael J. Foy

All characters appearing in this work are fictitious, Any resemblance to real persons, living or dead. The opinions expressed herein are those of the authors and not of MX Publishing.

Hardcover Casebound ISBN 9781787058255

Published by MX Publishing
335 Princess Park Manor, Royal Drive,
London, N11 3GX
www.mxpublishing.com

Cover design by Brian Belanger

I would like to thank Alexis Barquin for his help and encouragement and recommend his wonderful website https://www.arthur-conan-doyle.com.

Revised Edition 2022

Foreword

Mention the name Sherlock Holmes to anybody and they will almost instantly imagine a tall, clean-shaven person, with deerstalker, Calabash pipe and magnifying glass. He has become a true modern-day Icon, but this image of Holmes didn't come fully formed, It developed over time from book, newspaper and magazine illustrations as well as early stage and film portrayals. In this book and future ones, you will find, Sherlock Holmes with a beard, Sherlock Holmes with a moustache, a young and ultimately an old Holmes. But how best to organised this work, originally I was going to have all the illustrators listed in alphabetic order, so we would start with Stanley E. Armstrong in volume 1 and end with H. M. Wolcott in say volume 4, but, since the most famous illustrator* of Sherlock Holmes was Sidney Paget, readers would have had to wait until Volume 3 before any of his magnificent work appeared, which would have been a treat far too long delayed. I could have listed the illustrations in chronological order, but since this was meant to be a book about the artists, splitting their work over many volumes didn't seem right either. Instead this book will throw away convention, so you get a work that is neither alphabetic nor Chronological in order and just give you what you want mainly (certainly in this volume anyway) end to end Sidney Paget images. But just as the main course in a restaurant is delayed by an appetiser, we will start with a few early illustrations, then we show all 355 Sidney Paget's Sherlock Holmes ones. I have attributed all 'graphics' that appeared in the Strand Magazine in his section, so 'written letters', maps and of course the Dancing men will be included in the Sidney Paget illustrations section, they were probably composed by Sir Arthur Conan Doyle himself, but I am not going to apologise for their inclusion, they appeared in the relevant Strand Magazine and need to be included and this is the best place to put them.

I have endeavoured to find the best quality illustrations, converted them to Grayscale and adjusted levels to try to make them pop.
In subsequent volumes, I hope to include at least 78 other illustrators including the 1930's Leo O'Mealia Sherlock Holmes cartoon strip if copyright permission can be obtained, as well as foreign language works that were illustrated in journals and books around the World. Now it is true that sometimes these artists were 'greatly inspired' by Sidney Paget's work, sometimes to a point, shall we say of counterfeiting, these images could have been included in a 'Spot the difference puzzle', but more of that in volume 2. Foreign Sherlock Holmes illustrators we simply have to include later will be from Martin Van Maéle, Gaston Simoes da Fonseca and Josef Friedrich as well as many others.

My reluctance to spend time reading Sherlock Holmes stories from the privacy of a prison cell, forces me to deal with the thorny issue of Copyright, and particularly obtaining it in order to include some of the later Sherlock Holmes illustrations. Tracking down the owners, be they individuals or companies is proving difficult and since the Copyright laws differ from country to country, and we really need Worldwide permission in order to compile a definitive resource of Sherlock Holmes artwork is proving tricky. Some publishers are still in existence, while others have been swallowed by bigger corporations, who may or may not know copyright answers. So I am going to use my Foreword to send out a request to all Sherlock Holmes image artists or copyright owners of the same, to please contact me on the email below so that their work can be included in later volumes or the shake a fist at me and say 'keep your hands off' and if you are thinking that I wouldn't be interesting in publishing 'your' images, you are wrong. I want this series of books to be the best complete collection of all images of Sherlock Holmes and Sherlock Holmes stories, both Canon and parody, pastiche, cartoon, poster or painting. If it's an image of Sherlock Holmes, it is of interest to me. Traditional or contemporary. I just request that it has been a piece of work that has appeared in printed format of some kind elsewhere, not a doodle on the back of a packet of cigarettes. My email is listed at the bottom of the page.

As all early Sherlock Holmes work first appeared in black and white, this and perhaps the next volume will be exclusively B&W in order to keep the costs down. There will be colour volumes of this book, Frederic Door Steele's coloured images on the Cover of Collier's need to be seen in their original format and I have to include Sherlock Holmes Stamps too. Volume 3 is likely to be in colour.

So to sum up, this is a work in progress, some volumes will be in colour other black and white, I am open to all forms of Sherlock Holmes images, please do get in touch with me. In addition it would be nice to include some contemporary artists, who would like to showcase their work and show how Sherlock Holmes appears in the 21st century and perhaps even beyond.

Feedback is ALWAYS welcome, and changes are made when I screw things up, which happens regularly.

Anyway enjoy the first volume.

.

Mike Foy, Florida.

please contacted me at SherlockHolmesImages@gmail.com

* Some would argue that Frederic Dorr Steele is much more famous and there is some merit in this argument, Mr. Steele produced some very good illustrations for Collier's Magazine. (160 in total) and will be featuring prominently in a colour Volume soon, copyright permissions allowing.

News Flash, there is now an accompanying Facebook group called Sherlock Holmes - A Study in Illustrations. –

Index

The Bristol Observer

The Bristol Observer was a British Daily newspaper, which serialised the two stories A Study in Scarlet and The Sign of Four. Interestingly, they published the first two stories in reverse order. The Sign of Four appeared in eight issues every Saturday from 17th May 1890 until the 5th July 1890. A Study in Scarlet came out every Saturday over seven issues from the 18th October 1890 until the 29th November 1890. Each issue had 3 illustrations. 24 illustrations for the Sign of Four and 21 illustrations for A Study in Scarlet. Unfortunately the artist is unknown and because these images appeared in a newspaper, they are basic compared to later work. There are 45 illustrations in total.

The Bristol Observer - The Sign of Four Story 24 illustrations in 8 strips of 3.

Sign Part 1 out of 8, Saturday 17th May 1890

Sherlock Holmes
Ref. SH-TBO1

Holmes and Watson
Ref. SH-TBO2

Mary Morstan consults with Holmes
Ref. SH-TBO3

Sign Part 2 out of 8, Saturday 24th May 1890

One *Ref. SH-TBO1* of the Sikhs
Ref. SH-TBO4

Mary Morstan meeting Williams
Ref. SH-TBO5

Lal Chowdar with the Sholtos
Ref. SH-TBO6

Sign Part 3 out of 8, Saturday 31st May 1890

Arriving at Pondicherry Lodge, they meet McMurdo
Ref. SH-TBO7

Holmes discovers a dead Bartholomew Sholto
Ref. SH-TBO8

Holmes inspects the room above Sholto's study
Ref. SH-TBO9

Sign Part 4 out of 8, Saturday 7th June 1890

Toby the dog
Ref. SH-TBO10

Watson visits Mr. Sherman to collect Toby
Ref. SH-TBO11

Holmes (in deerstalker), Watson and Toby
Ref. SH-TBO12

Sign   Part 5 out of 8, Saturday 14th June 1890

The Baker Street Irregulars
Ref. SH-TBO13

Holmes and Watson meet with Mordecai Smith's wife and son Jack
Ref. SH-TBO14

Holmes in disguise plays a trick on Athelney Jones and Watson
Ref. SH-TBO15

Sign   Part 6 out of 8, Saturday 21st June 1890

Chapter 10 image of Jonathan Small
Ref. SH-TBO16

Jonathan Small and Tonga trying to escape
Ref. SH-TBO17

Watson takes the treasure chest around to Mary Morstan
Ref. SH-TBO18

Sign Part 7 out of 8, Saturday 28th June 1890

Achmet the Merchant arrives at Agra Fort
Ref. SH-TBO19

Jonathan Small tells his tale
Ref. SH-TBO20

Attack upon Achmet
Ref. SH-TBO21

Sign Part 8 out of 8, Saturday 5th July 1890

The Treasure of Agra
Ref. SH-TBO22

Abdullah, Akbar and Small bury Achmet
Ref. SH-TBO23

Small escapes from the prison on Blair Island
Ref. SH-TBO24

A Study in Scarlet appeared in the Bristol Observer from 18th October 1890 until 29th November 1890

The Bristol Observer – A Study in Scarlet 21 illustrations in 7 strips of 3.

Stud Part 1 out of 7, Saturday 18th October 1890

Stamford & Watson at Criterion
Ref. SH-TBO25

Stamford & Watson meeting Sherlock Holmes
Ref. SH-TBO26

Holmes & Watson at 221b Baker Street
Ref. SH-TBO27

Stud Part 2 out of 7, Saturday 25th October 1890

Rache, written on the wall
Ref. SH-TBO28

Holmes and Watson examine Enoch J. Drebber's dead body
Ref. SH-TBO29

John Rance answering Holmes and Watson's questions
Ref. SH-TBO30

Stud Part 3 out of 7, Saturday 1st November 1890

Wiggins and the street urchins
Ref. SH-TBO31

Watson and Mrs. Sawyer
Ref. SH-TBO32

Arthur, Alice and Madame Charpentier
Ref. SH-TBO33

Stud Part 4 out of 7, Saturday 8th November 1890

Light in this Darkness
Ref. SH-TBO34

Arrest of Jefferson Hope
Ref. SH-TBO35

John and Lucy Ferrier
Ref. SH-TBO36

Stud Part 5 out of 7, Saturday 15th November 1890

Lucy and John Ferrier
Ref. SH-TBO37

Lucy Ferrier and Jefferson Hope
Ref. SH-TBO38

Brigham Young and John Ferrier *Ref. SH-TBO39*

Stud Part 6 out of 7, Saturday 22nd November 1890

John Ferrier
Ref. SH-TBO40

John Ferrier, Joseph Stangerson and Enoch J. Drebber
Ref. SH-TBO41

Jefferson Hope discovers Lucy dead
Ref. SH-TBO42

Stud Part 7 out of 7, Saturday 29th November 1890

A continuation of the Reminiscences of John Watson MD
Ref. SH-TBO43

Fight between Enoch J Drebber and Jefferson Hope
Ref. SH-TBO44

Joseph Stangerson's dead body
Ref. SH-TBO45

Doyle, Charles Altamont

Charles Altamont Doyle (25th March 1832 – 10th October 1893) was an artist, watercolourist and illustrator, and the father of Arthur Conan Doyle. Charles illustrated a number of works including John Bunyan's Pilgrim's Progress and produced several illustrations for London Society between 1862 and 1864. References in the Sherlock Holmes story, where Watson talks about his Brother's life may have related to Conan Doyle's real father who never met with any success and fell into depression and alcoholism. Charles finally went insane and was interned in various asylums for the final 8 years of his life. His best artistic work are said to have been produced while in the asylums.

In July 1888, Charles did 6 illustrations for his son's novel A Study in Scarlet published by Ward, Lock & Co.,

Image of Charles Altamont Doyle and young son Sir Arthur Conan Doyle

Charles Altamont Doyle – A Study in Scarlet 6 illustrations

A Study in Scarlet July 1888 novel

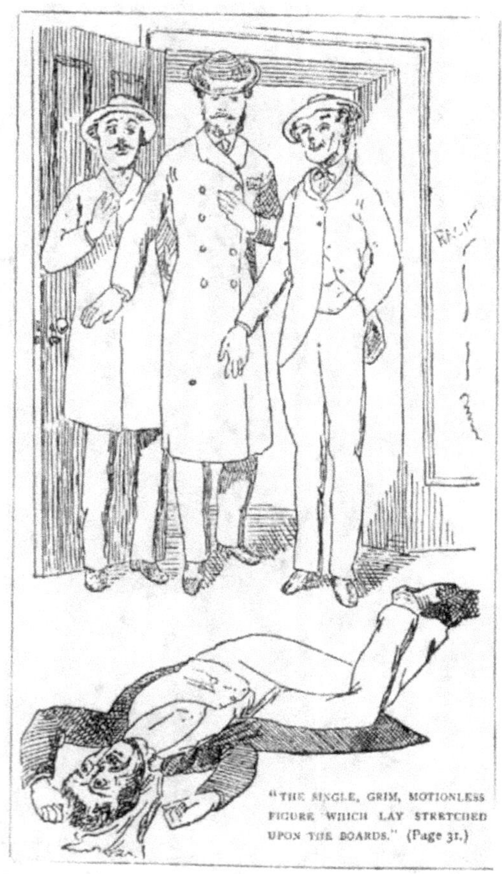

"THE SINGLE, GRIM, MOTIONLESS FIGURE WHICH LAY STRETCHED UPON THE BOARDS." (Page 31.)

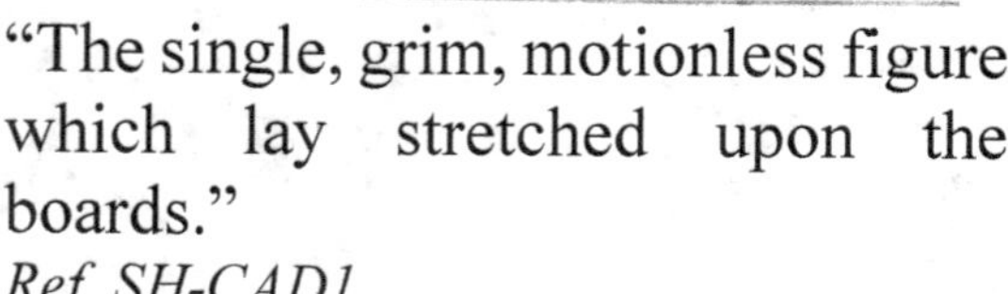

"The single, grim, motionless figure which lay stretched upon the boards."
Ref. SH-CAD1

Sherlock Holmes, Dr. Watson and the Baker Street Irregulars
Ref. SH-CAD2

A Study in Scarlet July 1888 novel

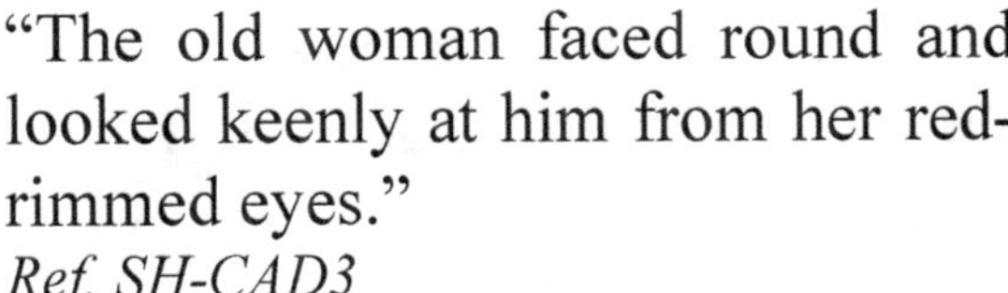

"The old woman faced round and looked keenly at him from her red-rimmed eyes."
Ref. SH-CAD3

"On the ledge of rock above this strange couple there stood three solemn buzzards."
Ref. SH-CAD4

"They had sat down to their breakfast, when Lucy with a cry of surprise pointed upwards. In the centre of the ceiling was scrawled, with a burned stick apparently, the number 28."
Ref. SH-CAD5

Enoch J. Drebber recognises the cabman as his old nemesis Jefferson Hope.
Ref. SH-CAD6

Friston, David Henry

David Henry Friston (1820-1906) was a British illustrator and figure painter. He is famous as the illustrator of the first Sherlock Holmes story in Beeton's Christmas Annual November 1887. He completed 4 Sherlock Holmes Illustrations.

Also Illustrated Gilbert & Sullivan reviews.

The following four images are illustrations from the Beeton's Annual.

Image details

- First ever image of Dr. Watson and Sherlock Holmes along with Scotland yard Inspectors G. Lestrade and Tobias Gregson. Lestrade is showing everyone the word he had discovered written on the wall at 3, Lauriston Gardens.
- Lestrade and Gregson look at each other as Sherlock Holmes looks at the body of Enoch J. Drebber.
- Jefferson Hope's story tells the tale of Lucy Ferrier and how she and her Adopted father, John Ferrier were rescued from certain death, when they are discovered alone on the Great Alkali Plain by a wagon train of Mormons looking for a place to live.
- The final image shows Jefferson Hope as he crawls into the home of Lucy and John Ferrier before they try to escape.

Friston, David Henry - A Study in Scarlet 4 illustrations

Dr. Watson, Sherlock Holmes, G. Lestrade and Gregson

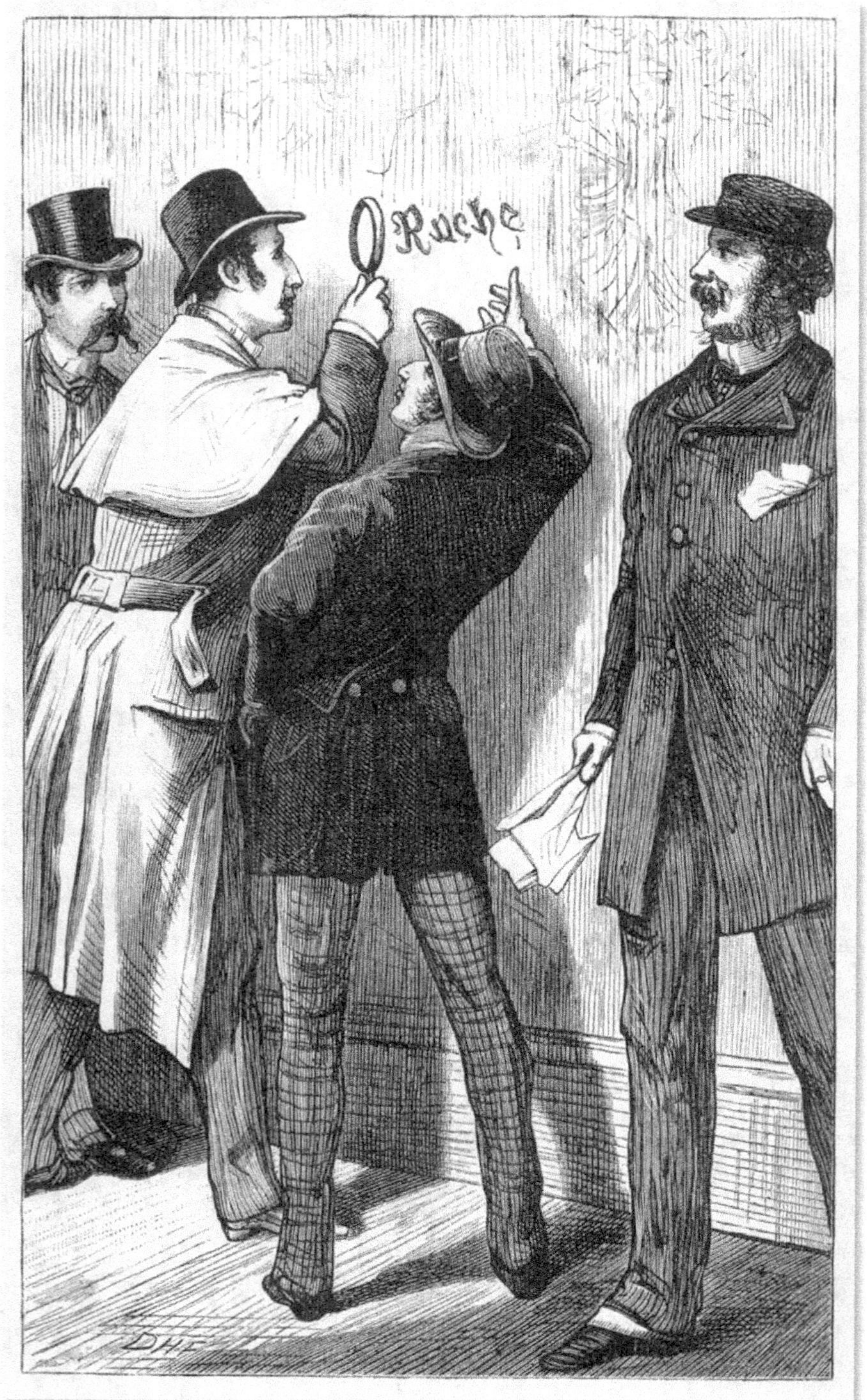

"He examined with his glass the word upon the wall, going over every letter of it with the most minute exactness."

Ref. SH-DHF1

G. Lestrade, Tobias Gregson, Sherlock Holmes and the dead Enoch J. Drebber

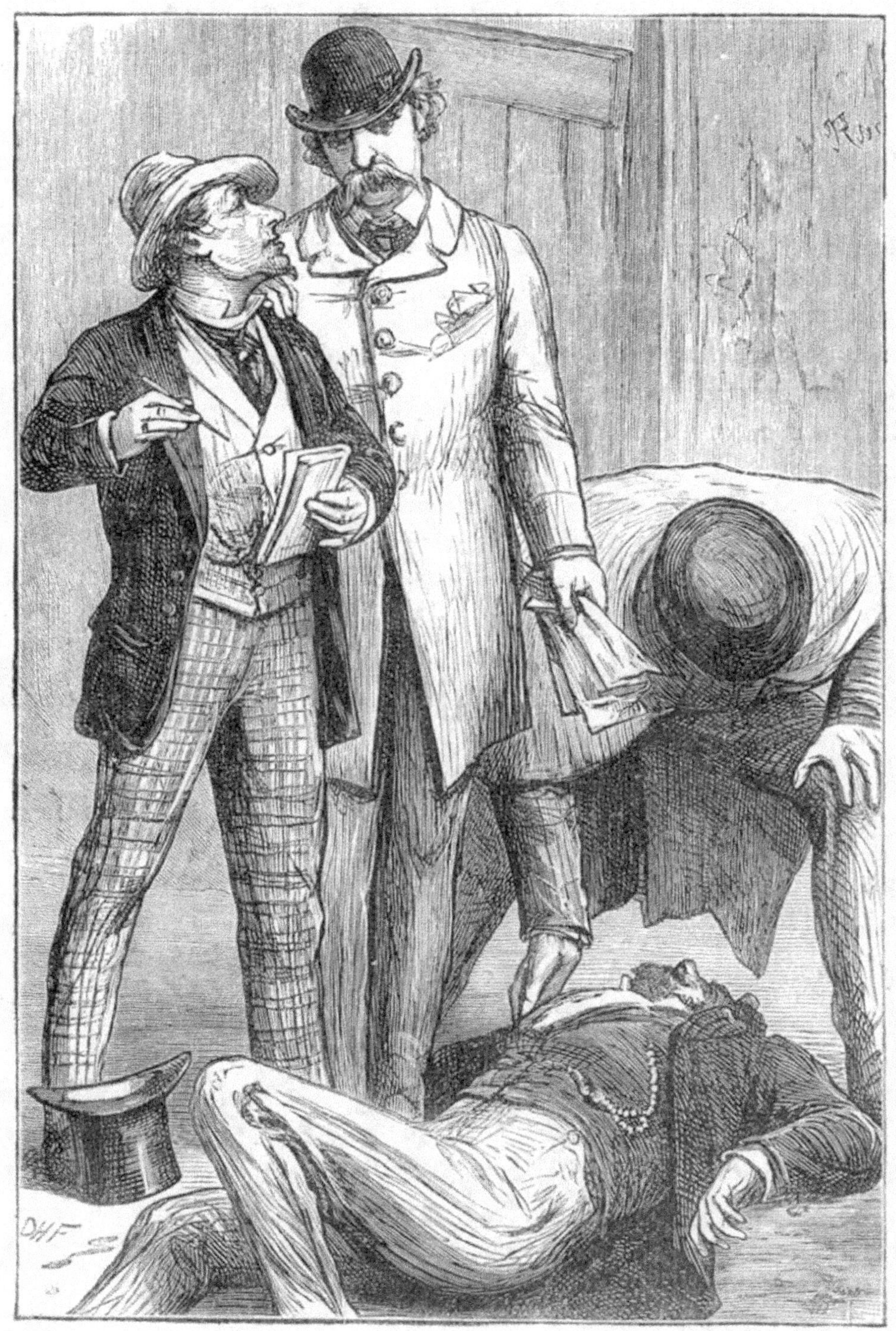

"As he spoke, his nimble fingers were flying here, there, and everywhere."
Ref. SH-DHF2

John and Lucy Ferrier are rescued by a wagon train of Mormons

"One of them seized the little girl, and hoisted her upon his shoulder."
Ref. SH-DHF3

Jefferson Hope arrives at John Ferrier's surrounded Farm

"As he watched it he saw it writhe along the ground."
Ref. SH-DHF4

Greig, James

James Greig (1861-1941) was a British illustrator, well known for his regular illustrations in The Strand Magazine.

He produced two illustrations for A Study in Scarlet in December 1895 & 1896

The 1895 illustration appeared in The Windsor Magazine supplement and the 1896 one was in a new Ward Lock & Co. Book.

Greig James – A Study in Scarlet. 1895 1 illustration

A Study in Scarlet   Windsor Magazine Supplement December 1895

"Sherlock Holmes approached the body."

Ref. SH-JG1

Greig, James – A Study in Scarlet 1896 Book.

"United in the entreaty for mercy."

Ref. SH-JG2

Paget, Sidney Edward

Born 4th October 1860 in London, Died 28th January 1908 in Margate. The story of how Sidney Paget became the most famous Sherlock Holmes illustrator is fascinating (if only it were true).

In 1890, the publisher George Newnes, started a new monthly magazine, that he called 'The Strand', The first issued appeared in December 1890, but was actually dated January 1891. The magazine proved very popular and would soon become famous in the Sherlock Holmes lore when the Holmes' first short story called 'A Scandal in Bohemia' came out in July 1891, more stories would follow, and the first 12 of these would reappear later in a collection called 'The Adventures of Sherlock Holmes'. The Story goes:

Once upon a time there were three brothers*, called Henry Marriott, the eldest, Sidney and the youngest Walter, all were Pagets. Newnes wanted an illustrator and asked his art director W.H. Boot, to find someone, Boot sent a letter to Walter asking for him to illustrate Arthur Conan Doyle's new story and by some strange hand of fate, Sidney got hold of the letter and was the one who ended up with the commission and the fame. An interesting story but recent research has cast doubt on this story. It was also said that although Walter lost out on the commission, his brother used him for the likeliness of Holmes. This was denied by Henry Marriott, but I ask you to look at the Walter Paget section and see if you find they do look similar.

He died in Margate at the age of 47, and his death certificate shows he died from a Mediastinal tumour. He was buried in East Finchley cemetery.

*Sidney was the fifth of nine.

356 Illustrations in 38 stories

	Name	images	The Strand Magazine date
1	A Scandal in Bohemia	10	July 1891
2	The Red-Headed League	10	August 1891
3	A Case of Identity	7	September 1891
4	The Boscombe Valley Mystery	10	October 1891
5	The Five Orange Pips	6	November 1891
6	The Man with the Twisted Lip	10	December 1891
7	The Adventure of the Blue Carbuncle	8	January 1982
8	The Adventure of the Speckled Band	`9	February 1892
9	The Adventure of the Engineer's Thumb	8	March 1892
10	The Adventure of the Noble Bachelor	8	April 1892
11	The Adventure of the Beryl Coronet	9	May 1892
12	The Adventure of the Copper Beeches	9	June 1892
13	The Adventure of the Silver Blaze	9	December 1892
14	The Adventure of the Cardboard Box	8	January 1893
15	The Adventure of the Yellow Face	7	February 1893
16	The Adventure of the Stockbroker's Clerk	7	March 1893
17	The Adventure of the Gloria Scot	7	April 1893
18	The Adventure of the Musgrave Ritual	6	May 1893
19	The Adventure of the Reigate Squire	7	June 1893
20	The Adventure of the Crooked Man	7	July 1893
21	The Adventure of the Resident Patient	7	August 1893
22	The Adventure of the Greek Interpreter	8	September 1893
23	The Adventure of the Naval Treaty 1 +2	8+7	Oct-Nov 1893
24	The Adventure of the Final Problem	9	December 1893
25	The Hound of the Baskervilles (7+8+7+7+6+7+4+7+7)	60	Aug1901-Apr1902
26	The Adventure of the Empty House	7	October 1903
27	The Adventure of the Norwood Builder	7	November 1903
28	The Adventure of the Dancing Men	7	December 1903
29	The Adventure of the Solitary Cyclist	7	January 1904
30	The Adventure of the Priory School	9	February 1904
31	The Adventure of Black Peter	7	March 1904
32	The Adventure of Charles Augustus Milverton	6	April 1904
33	The Adventure of the Six Napoleons	7	May 1904
34	The Adventure of the Three Students	7	June 1904
35	The Adventure of the Golden Pince-Nez	8	July 1904
36	The Adventure of the Missing Three-Quarter	7	August 1904
37	The Adventure of the Abbey Grange	8	September 1904
38	The Adventure of the Second Stain	8	October 1904

Sidney Paget – A Scandal in Bohemia. The Strand Magazine Page 62. July 1891. 10 illustrations.

Image 1/10. "Then he stood before the fire."
Ref. SH-SP1

Sidney Paget – A Scandal in Bohemia. The Strand Magazine Page 63. July 1891. 10 illustrations.

Image 2/10. “I carefully examined the writing.”
Ref. SH-SP2

Sidney Paget – A Scandal in Bohemia. The Strand Magazine Page 64. July 1891. 10 illustrations.

Image 3/10. p 64. “A man entered.”
Ref. SH-SP3

Sidney Paget – A Scandal in Bohemia. The Strand Magazine Page 65. July 1891. 10 illustrations.

Image 4/10. "He tore the mask from his face."
Ref. SH-SP4

Sidney Paget – A Scandal in Bohemia. The Strand Magazine Page 67. July 1891. 10 illustrations.

Image 5/10. "A drunken-looking Groom."
Ref. SH-SP5

Sidney Paget – A Scandal in Bohemia. The Strand Magazine Page 69. July 1891. 10 illustrations.

Image 6/10. "I found myself mumbling responses."
Ref. SH-SP6

Sidney Paget – A Scandal in Bohemia. The Strand Magazine Page. 70 July 1891. 10 illustrations.

Image 7/10. “A simple minded clergyman.”
Ref. SH-SP7

Sidney Paget – A Scandal in Bohemia. The Strand Magazine Page 71. July 1891. 10 illustrations.

Image 8/10. "He gave a cry and dropped."
Ref. SH-SP8

Sidney Paget – A Scandal in Bohemia. The Strand Magazine Page 73. July 1891. 10 illustrations.

Image 9/10. "Good-night, Mr. Sherlock Holmes."
Ref. SH-SP9

Sidney Paget – A Scandal in Bohemia. The Strand Magazine Page 74. July 1891. 10 illustrations.

Image 10/10. "This photograph!"
Ref. SH-SP10

Sidney Paget – The Red-Headed League. The Strand Magazine Page 190. August 1891. 10 illustrations.

Image 1/10. Mr. Jabez Wilson
Ref. SH-SP11

Sidney Paget – The Red-Headed League. The Strand Magazine Page 192. August 1891. 10 illustrations.

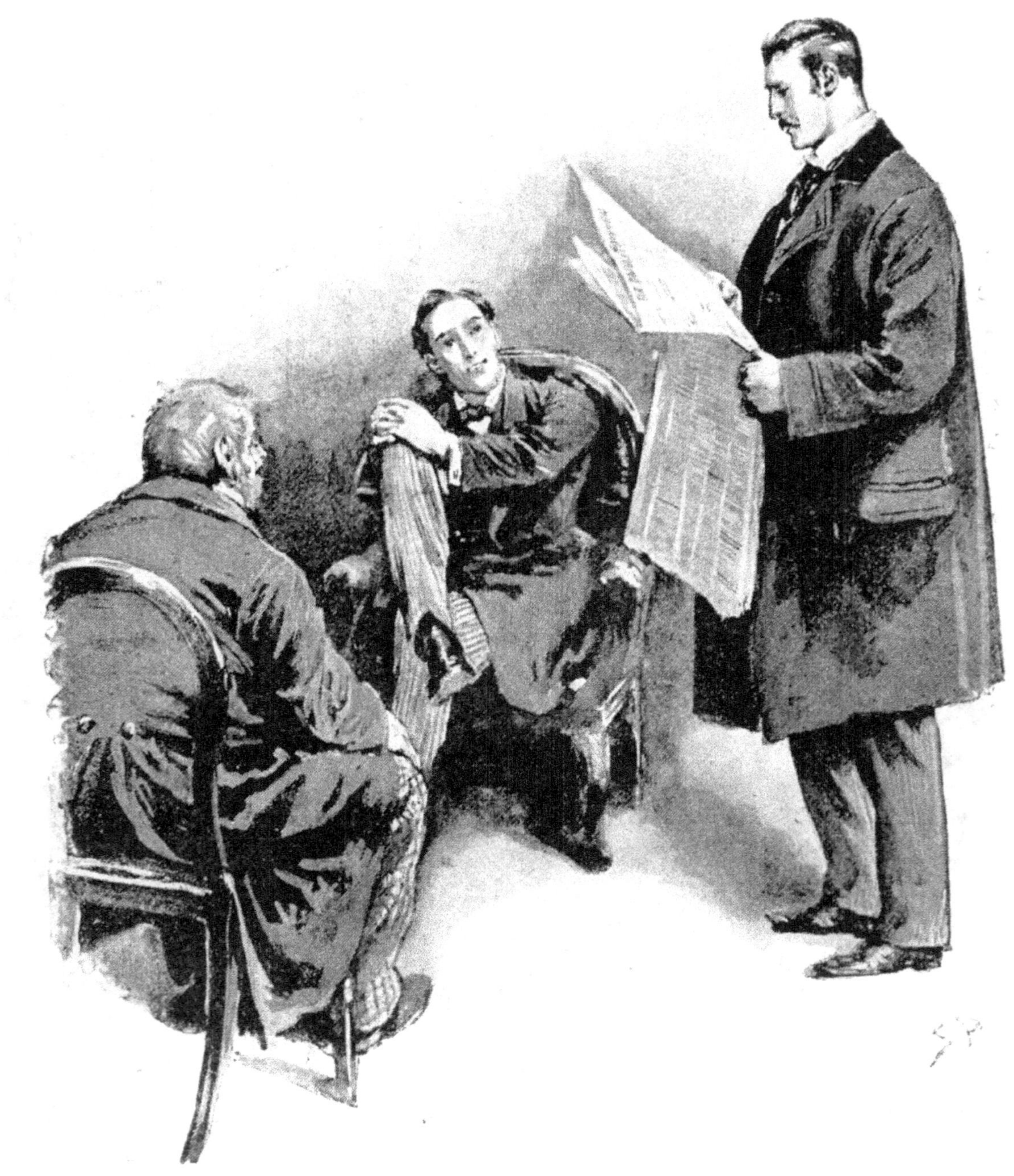

Image 2/10. "What on Earth does this mean?"
Ref. SH-SP12

Sidney Paget – The Red-Headed League. The Strand Magazine Page 193. August 1891. 10 illustrations.

Image 3/10. “The League has a vacancy.”
Ref. SH-SP13

Sidney Paget – The Red-Headed League. The Strand Magazine Page 194. August 1891. 10 illustrations.

Image 4/10. “He congratulated me warmly.”
Ref. SH-SP14

Sidney Paget – The Red-Headed League. The Strand Magazine Page 196. August 1891. 10 illustrations.

Image 5/10. “The door was shut and locked.”
Ref. SH-SP15

Sidney Paget – The Red-Headed League. The Strand Magazine Page 197. August 1891. 10 illustrations.

Image 6/10. "He curled himself up in his chair."
Ref. SH-SP16

Sidney Paget – The Red-Headed League. The Strand Magazine Page 198. August 1891. 10 illustrations.

Image 7/10. "The Door was instantly opened."
Ref. SH-SP17

Sidney Paget – The Red-Headed League. The Strand Magazine Page 199. August 1891. 10 illustrations.

Image 8/10. “All afternoon he sat in the stalls.”
Ref. SH-SP18

Sidney Paget – The Red-Headed League. The Strand Magazine Page 201. August 1891. 10 illustrations.

Image 9/10. "Mr. Merryweather stopped to light a lantern."
Ref. SH-SP19

Sidney Paget – The Red-Headed League. The Strand Magazine Page 203. August 1891. 10 illustrations.

Image 10/10. "It's no use, John Clay."
Ref. SH-SP20

Sidney Paget – The Case of Identity. The Strand Magazine Page 249. September 1891. 7 illustrations.

Image 1/7. "Sherlock Holmes Welcomed her."
Ref. SH-SP21

Sidney Paget – The Case of Identity. The Strand Magazine Page 251. September 1891. 7 illustrations.

Image 2/7. “At the Gasfitters’ ball.”
Ref. SH-SP22

Sidney Paget – The Case of Identity. The Strand Magazine Page 252. September 1891. 7 illustrations.

Image 3/7. "There was no one there."
Ref. SH-SP23

Sidney Paget – The Case of Identity. The Strand Magazine Page 253. September 1891. 7 illustrations.

Image 4/7. "She laid a little bundle upon the table."
Ref. SH-SP24

Sidney Paget – The Case of Identity. The Strand Magazine Page 255 September 1891. 7 illustrations.

Image 5/7. "I found Sherlock Holmes half asleep."
Ref. SH-SP25

Sidney Paget – The Case of Identity. The Strand Magazine Page 257. September 1891. 7 illustrations.

Image 6/7. “Glancing about him like a rat in a trap.”
Ref. SH-SP26

Sidney Paget – The Case of Identity. The Strand Magazine Page 258. September 1891. 7 illustrations.

Image 7/7. "He took two swift steps to the whip."
Ref. SH-SP27

Sidney Paget – The Boscombe Valley Mystery. The Strand Magazine Page 401. October 1891. 10 illustrations.

Image 1/10. “We had the carriage to ourselves.”
Ref. SH-SP28

Sidney Paget – The Boscombe Valley Mystery. The Strand Magazine Page 403. October 1891. 10 illustrations.

Image 2/10. "They found the body."
Ref. SH-SP29

Sidney Paget – The Boscombe Valley Mystery. The Strand Magazine Page 405 October 1891. 10 illustrations.

Image 3/10. “I held him in my arms.”
Ref. SH-SP30

Sidney Paget – The Boscombe Valley Mystery. The Strand Magazine Page 407. October 1891. 10 illustrations.

Image 4/10. "Lestrade shrugged his shoulders."
Ref. SH-SP31

Sidney Paget – The Boscombe Valley Mystery. The Strand Magazine Page 408. October 1891. 10 illustrations.

Image 5/10. "I tried to interest myself in a yellow-backed novel."
Ref. SH-SP32

Sidney Paget – The Boscombe Valley Mystery. The Strand Magazine Page 410. October 1891. 10 illustrations.

Image 6/10. "The maid showed us the boots."
Ref. SH-SP33

Sidney Paget – The Boscombe Valley Mystery. The Strand Magazine Page 411. October 1891. 10 illustrations.

Image 7/10. “For a long time he remained there.”
Ref. SH-SP34

Sidney Paget – The Boscombe Valley Mystery. The Strand Magazine Page 412. October 1891. 10 illustrations.

Image 8/10. "He had stood behind that tree."
Ref. SH-SP35

Sidney Paget – The Boscombe Valley Mystery. The Strand Magazine Page 413. October 1891. 10 illustrations.

Image 9/10. “Mr. John Turner,” said the waiter.
Ref. SH-SP36

Sidney Paget – The Boscombe Valley Mystery. The Strand Magazine Page 415. October 1891. 10 illustrations.

Image 10/10. " 'Farewell, then,' said the old man."
Ref. SH-SP37

Sidney Paget – The Five Orange Pips The Strand Magazine Page 482. November 1891. 6 illustrations.

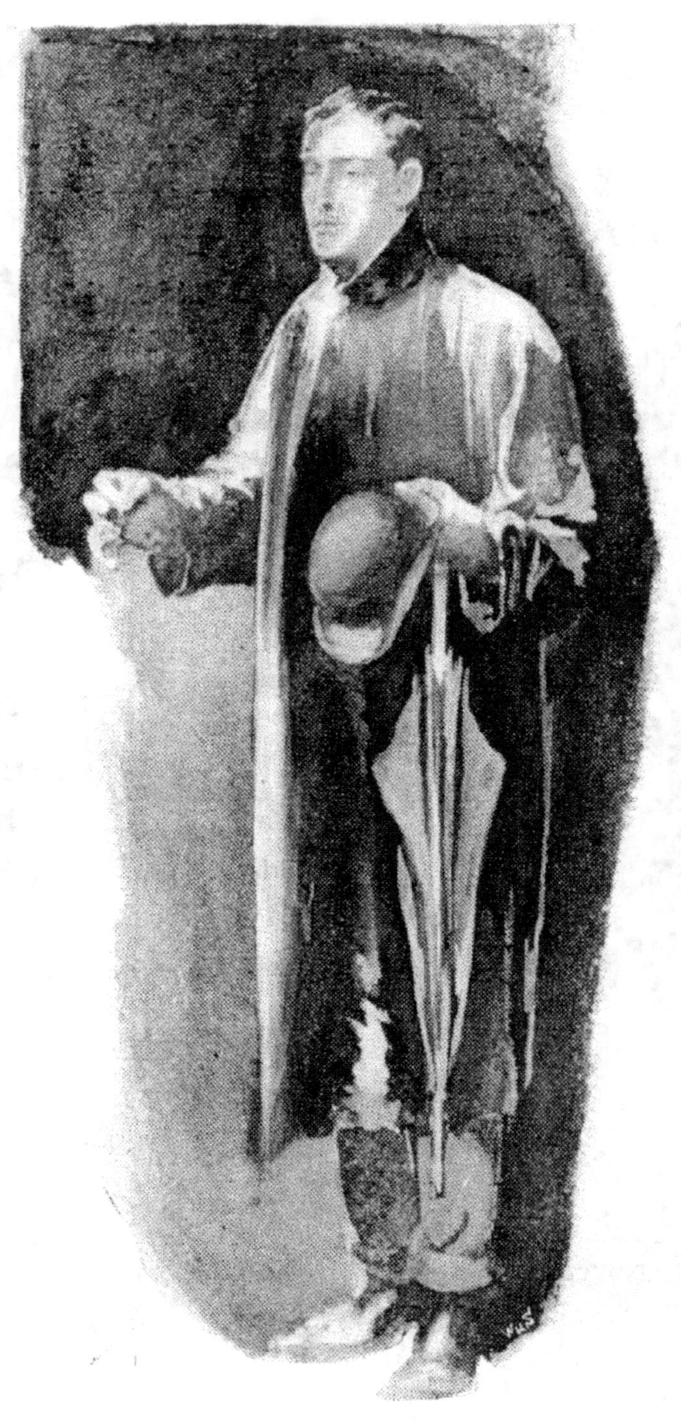

Image 1/6. "He looked about him anxiously"
Ref. SH-SP38

Sidney Paget – The Five Orange Pips. The Strand Magazine Page 484. November 1891. 6 illustrations.

Image 2/6. "We found him face downwards in a little green scummed pool."
Ref. SH-SP39

Sidney Paget – The Five Orange Pips. The Strand Magazine Page 485. November 1891. 6 illustrations.

Image 3/6. "What on Earth does this mean?"
Ref. SH-SP40

Sidney Paget – The Five Orange Pips. The Strand Magazine Page 486. November 1891. 6 illustrations.

Image 4/6. "Shook out five little dried orange pips. "
Ref. SH-SP41

Sidney Paget – The Five Orange Pips. The Strand Magazine Page 488. November 1891. 6 illustrations.

Image 5/6. "His eyes bent upon the glow of the fire."
Ref. SH-SP42

Sidney Paget – The Five Orange Pips. The Strand Magazine Page 490. November 1891. 6 illustrations.

Image 6/6. "Holmes. " I cried, "You are too late."
Ref. SH-SP43

Sidney Paget – The Man with Twisted Lip. The Strand Magazine Page. 624. December 1891. 10 illustrations.

Image 1/10. “Staring into the fire.”
Ref. SH-SP44

Sidney Paget – The Man with Twisted Lip. The Strand Magazine Page 625. December 1891. 10 illustrations.

Image 2/10. " 'Holmes!' I whispered."
Ref. SH-SP45

Sidney Paget – The Man with Twisted Lip. The Strand Magazine Page 626. December 1891. 10 illustrations.

Image 3/10. “He flicked the horse with a whip.”
Ref. SH-SP46

Sidney Paget – The Man with Twisted Lip. The Strand Magazine Page 628. December 1891. 10 illustrations.

Image 4/10. " At the foot of the stairs she met this lascar scoundrel."
Ref. SH-SP47

Sidney Paget – The Man with Twisted Lip. The Strand Magazine Page 629. December 1891. 10 illustrations.

Image 5/10. " A professional beggar."
Ref. SH-SP48

Sidney Paget – The Man with Twisted Lip. The Strand Magazine Page 630. December 1891. 10 illustrations.

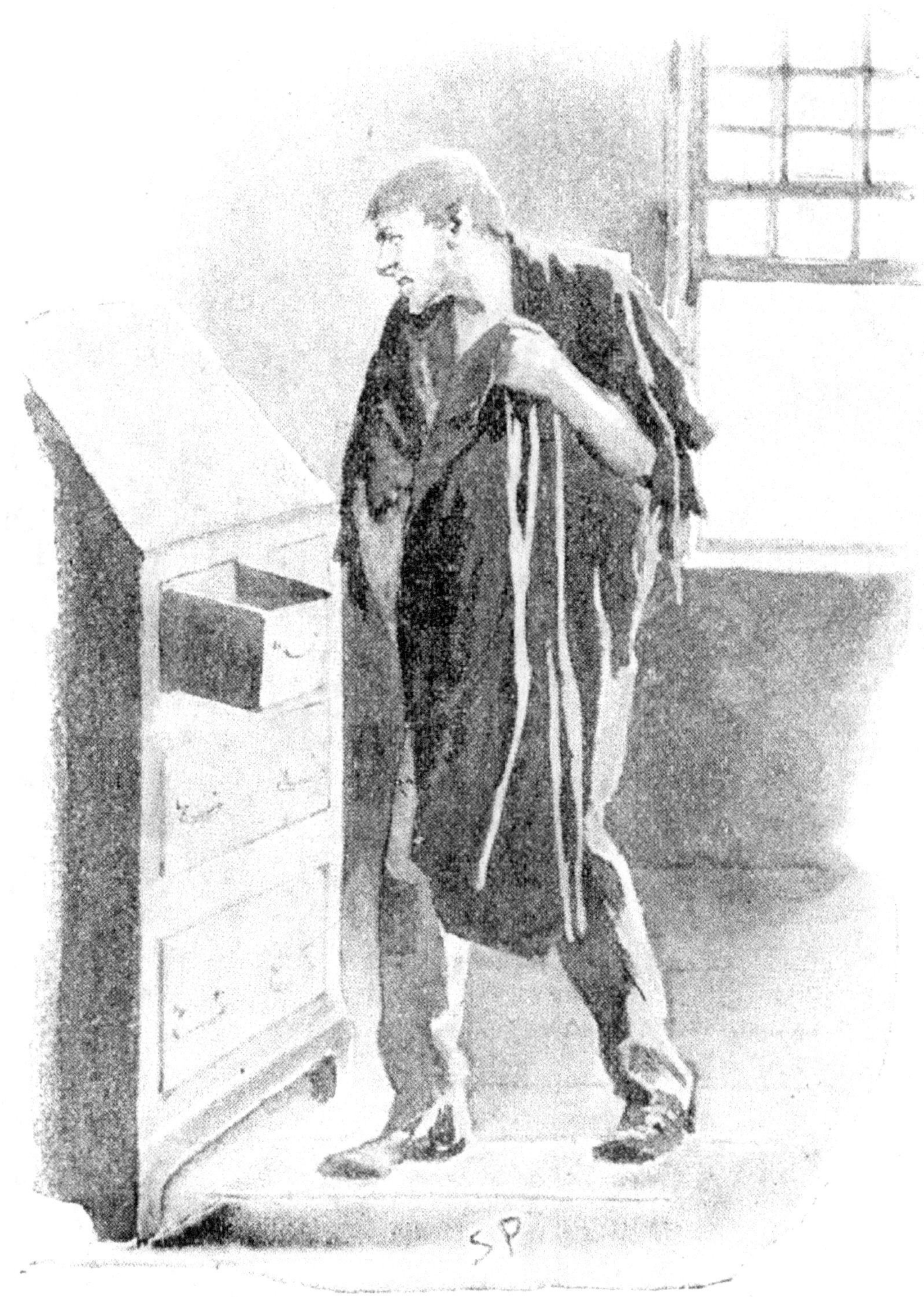

Image 6/10. " Stuffs all the coins into the pockets."
Ref. SH-SP49

Sidney Paget – The Man with Twisted Lip. The Strand Magazine Page 632. December 1891. 10 illustrations.

Image 7/10. " 'Frankly, now,' she repeated."
Ref. SH-SP50

Sidney Paget – The Man with Twisted Lip. The Strand Magazine Page 634. December 1891. 10 illustrations.

Image 8/10. " The pipe was still between his lips."
Ref. SH-SP51

Sidney Paget – The Man with Twisted Lip. The Strand Magazine Page 635. December 1891. 10 illustrations.

Image 9/10. " He took out a very large bath sponge."
Ref. SH-SP52

Sidney Paget – The Man with Twisted Lip. The Strand Magazine Page 636. December 1891. 10 illustrations.

Image 10/10. "He broke into a scream."
Ref. SH-SP53

Sidney Paget – The Adventure of the Blue Carbuncle. The Strand Magazine Page 73. January 1892. 8 illustrations.

Image 1/8. " A very seedy hard felt hat."
Ref. SH-SP54

Sidney Paget – The Adventure of the Blue Carbuncle. The Strand Magazine Page 74. January 1892. 8 illustrations.

Image 2/8. " The roughs had fled at the appearance of Peterson."
Ref. SH-SP55

Sidney Paget – The Adventure of the Blue Carbuncle. The Strand Magazine Page 76. January 1892. 8 illustrations.

Image 3/8. " See what my wife found in its crop!"
Ref. SH-SP56

Sidney Paget – The Adventure of the Blue Carbuncle. The Strand Magazine Page 79. January 1892. 8 illustrations.

Image 4/8. " He bowed solemnly to both of us."
Ref. SH-SP57

Sidney Paget – The Adventure of the Blue Carbuncle. The Strand Magazine Page 81. January 1892. 8 illustrations.

Image 5/8. " Just read it out to me."
Ref. SH-SP58

Sidney Paget – The Adventure of the Blue Carbuncle. The Strand Magazine Page 82. January 1892. 8 illustrations.

Image 6/8. " You are the very man."
Ref. SH-SP59

Sidney Paget – The Adventure of the Blue Carbuncle. The Strand Magazine Page 83. January 1892. 8 illustrations.

Image 7/8. 'Have mercy!' he shrieked.
Ref. SH-SP60

Sidney Paget – The Adventure of the Blue Carbuncle. The Strand Magazine Page 85. January 1892. 8 illustrations.

Image 8/8. " He burst into convulsive sobbing."
Ref. SH-SP61

Sidney Paget – The Adventure of the Speckled Band. The Strand Magazine Page 143. February 1892. 9 illustrations.

Image 1/9. " She raised her veil."
Ref. SH-SP62

Sidney Paget – The Adventure of the Speckled Band. The Strand Magazine Page 144. February 1892. 9 illustrations.

Image 2/9. " He hurled the blacksmith over a parapet."
Ref. SH-SP63

Sidney Paget – The Adventure of the Speckled Band. The Strand Magazine Page 146. February 1892. 9 illustrations.

Image 3/8. " Her face blanched with terror."
Ref. SH-SP64

Sidney Paget – The Adventure of the Speckled Band. The Strand Magazine Page 148. February 1892. 9 illustrations.

Image 4/9. " Which of you is Holmes?"
Ref. SH-SP65

Sidney Paget – The Adventure of the Speckled Band. The Strand Magazine Page 150. February 1892. 9 illustrations.

Image 5/9. " We got off, paid our fare."
Ref. SH-SP66

Sidney Paget – The Adventure of the Speckled Band. The Strand Magazine Page 152. February 1892. 9 illustrations.

Image 6/9. " Well, look at this."
Ref. SH-SP67

Sidney Paget – The Adventure of the Speckled Band. The Strand Magazine Page 153. February 1892. 9 illustrations.

Image 7/9. " Good-bye, and be brave."
Ref. SH-SP68

Sidney Paget – The Adventure of the Speckled Band. The Strand Magazine Page 155. February 1892. 9 illustrations.

Image 8/9. " Holmes lashed furiously."
Ref. SH-SP69

Sidney Paget – The Adventure of the Speckled Band. The Strand Magazine Page 156. February 1892. 9 illustrations.

Image 9/9. " He made neither sound nor motion."
Ref. SH-SP70

Sidney Paget – The Adventure of the Engineer's Thumb. The Strand Magazine Page 277. March 1892. 8 illustrations.

Image 1/8. " He unwound the handkerchief, and held out his hand."
Ref. SH-SP71

Sidney Paget – The Adventure of the Engineer's Thumb. The Strand Magazine Page 278. March 1892. 8 illustrations.

Image 2/8. " He settled our new acquaintance on the sofa."
Ref. SH-SP72

Sidney Paget – The Adventure of the Engineer's Thumb. The Strand Magazine Page 279. March 1892. 8 illustrations.

Image 3/8. " Colonel Lysander Stark."
Ref. SH-SP73

Sidney Paget – The Adventure of the Engineer's Thumb. The Strand Magazine Page 281. March 1892. 8 illustrations.

Image 4/8. " Not a word to a soul!"
Ref. SH-SP74

Sidney Paget – The Adventure of the Engineer's Thumb. The Strand Magazine Page 283. March 1892. 8 illustrations.

Image 5/8. " 'Get away from here before it is too late.' "
Ref. SH-SP75

Sidney Paget – The Adventure of the Engineer's Thumb. The Strand Magazine Page 284. March 1892. 8 illustrations.

Image 6/8. " I rushed to the door."
Ref. SH-SP76

Sidney Paget – The Adventure of the Engineer's Thumb. The Strand Magazine Page 286. March 1892. 8 illustrations.

Image 7/8. " 'He cut at me.' "
Ref. SH-SP77

Sidney Paget – The Adventure of the Engineer's Thumb. The Strand Magazine Page 288. March 1892. 8 illustrations.

Image 8/8. " A house on fire?"
Ref. SH-SP78

Sidney Paget – The Adventure of the Noble Bachelor. The Strand Magazine Page 386. April 1892. 8 illustrations.

Image 1/8. " He broke the seal and glanced over the contents."
Ref. SH-SP79

Sidney Paget – The Adventure of the Noble Bachelor. The Strand Magazine Page 389. April 1892. 8 illustrations.

Image 2/8. " She was ejected by the butler and the footman ."
Ref. SH-SP80

Sidney Paget – The Adventure of the Noble Bachelor. The Strand Magazine Page 390. April 1892. 8 illustrations.

Image 3/8. " Lord Robert St. Simon ."
Ref. SH-SP81

Sidney Paget – The Adventure of the Noble Bachelor. The Strand Magazine Page 391. April 1892. 8 illustrations.

Image 4/8. " The gentleman in the pew handed it up to her."
Ref. SH-SP82

Sidney Paget – The Adventure of the Noble Bachelor. The Strand Magazine Page 393. April 1892. 8 illustrations.

Image 5/8. " 'There,' said he."
Ref. SH-SP83

Sidney Paget – The Adventure of the Noble Bachelor. The Strand Magazine Page 395. April 1892. 8 illustrations.

Image 6/8. A picture of offended dignity.
Ref. SH-SP84

Sidney Paget – The Adventure of the Noble Bachelor. The Strand Magazine Page 397. April 1892. 8 illustrations.

Image 7/8. "Some woman came talking about Lord St. Simon."
Ref. SH-SP85

Sidney Paget – The Adventure of the Noble Bachelor. The Strand Magazine Page 398. April 1892. 8 illustrations.

Image 8/8. " I will wish you all a very good night."
Ref. SH-SP86

Sidney Paget – The Adventure of the Beryl Coronet. The Strand Magazine Page 511. May 1892. 9 illustrations.

Image 1/9. " With a look of grief and despair."
Ref. SH-SP87

Sidney Paget – The Adventure of the Beryl Coronet. The Strand Magazine Page 513. May 1892. 9 illustrations.

Image 2/9. " I took the precious case."
Ref. SH-SP88

Sidney Paget – The Adventure of the Beryl Coronet. The Strand Magazine Page 515. May 1892. 9 illustrations.

Image 3/9. " Oh, any old key will fit that bureau."
Ref. SH-SP89

Sidney Paget – The Adventure of the Beryl Coronet. The Strand Magazine Page 516. May 1892. 9 illustrations.

Image 4/9. " At my cry he dropped it."
Ref. SH-SP90

Sidney Paget – The Adventure of the Beryl Coronet. The Strand Magazine Page 518. May 1892. 9 illustrations.

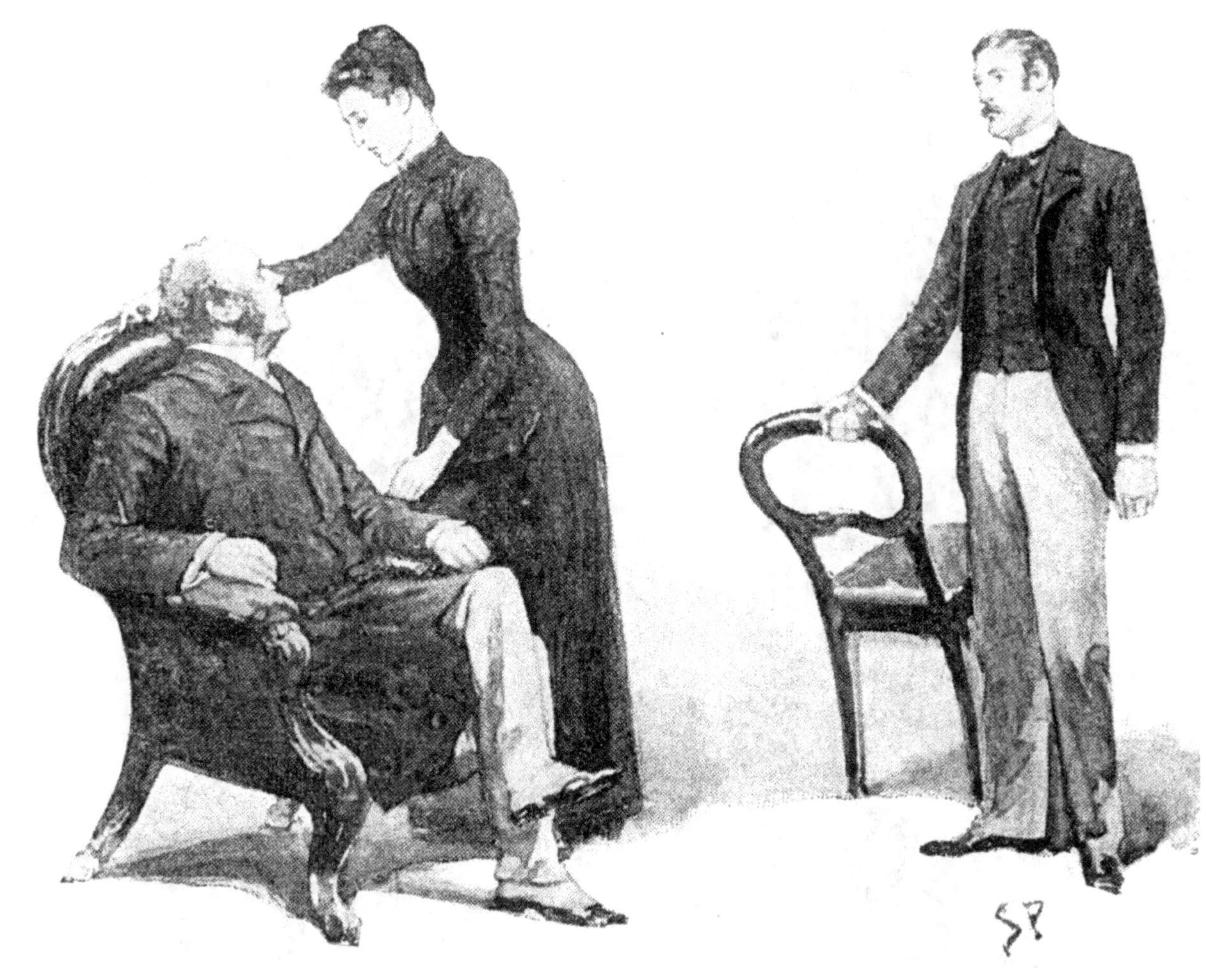

Image 5/9. " She went straight to her uncle."
Ref. SH-SP91

Sidney Paget – The Adventure of the Beryl Coronet. The Strand Magazine Page 519. May 1892. 9 illustrations.

Image 6/9. “ Something like fear sprang up in the young lady’s eyes.”
Ref. SH-SP92

Sidney Paget – The Adventure of the Beryl Coronet. The Strand Magazine Page 521. May 1892. 9 illustrations.

Image 7/9. " Dressed as a common loafer."
Ref. SH-SP93

Sidney Paget – The Adventure of the Beryl Coronet. The Strand Magazine Page 523. May 1892. 9 illustrations.

Image 8/9. "Arthur caught him."
Ref. SH-SP94

Sidney Paget – The Adventure of the Beryl Coronet. The Strand Magazine Page 525. May 1892. 9 illustrations.

Image 9/9. " I clapped a pistol to his head."
Ref. SH-SP95

Sidney Paget – The Adventure of the Copper Beeches. The Strand Magazine Page 613. Jun 1892. 9 illustrations.

Image 1/9. "Taking up a glowing cinder with the tongs."
Ref. SH-SP96

Sidney Paget – The Adventure of the Copper Beeches. The Strand Magazine Page 615. Jun 1892. 9 illustrations.

Image 2/9. "Capital."
Ref. SH-SP97

Sidney Paget – The Adventure of the Copper Beeches. The Strand Magazine Page 617. Jun 1892. 9 illustrations.

Image 3/9. "Holmes shook his head gravely."
Ref. SH-SP98

Sidney Paget – The Adventure of the Copper Beeches. The Strand Magazine Page 619. Jun 1892. 9 illustrations.

Image 4/9. "I am so delighted that you have come."
Ref. SH-SP99

Sidney Paget – The Adventure of the Copper Beeches. The Strand Magazine Page 621. Jun 1892. 9 illustrations.

Image 5/9. "I read for about ten minutes."
Ref. SH-SP100

Sidney Paget – The Adventure of the Copper Beeches. The Strand Magazine Page 622. Jun 1892. 9 illustrations.

Image 6/9. “I took it up and examined it.”
Ref. SH-SP101

Sidney Paget – The Adventure of the Copper Beeches. The Strand Magazine Page 624. Jun 1892. 9 illustrations.

Image 7/9. " 'Oh! I am so frightened!' I panted."
Ref. SH-SP102

Sidney Paget – The Adventure of the Copper Beeches. The Strand Magazine Page 626. Jun 1892. 9 illustrations.

Image 8/9. " 'You villain!' said he. 'Where's your daughter?' "
Ref. SH-SP103

Sidney Paget – The Adventure of the Copper Beeches. The Strand Magazine Page 627. Jun 1892. 9 illustrations.

Image 9/9. “Running up, I blew it’s brains out.”
Ref. SH-SP104

Sidney Paget – The Adventure of Silver Blaze. The Strand Magazine Page 646. December 1892. 9 illustrations.

Image 1/9. "Holmes gave me a sketch of the events."
Ref. SH-SP105

Sidney Paget – The Adventure of Silver Blaze. The Strand Magazine Page 647. December 1892. 9 illustrations.

Image 2/9. "A man appeared out of the darkness."
Ref. SH-SP106

Sidney Paget – The Adventure of Silver Blaze. The Strand Magazine Page 648. December 1892. 9 illustrations.

Image 3/9. “They found the dead body of the unfortunate trainer.”
Ref. SH-SP107

Sidney Paget – The Adventure of Silver Blaze. The Strand Magazine Page 650. December 1892. 9 illustrations.

Image 4/9. "I am delighted that you have come down, Mr. Holmes."
Ref. SH-SP108

Sidney Paget – The Adventure of Silver Blaze. The Strand Magazine Page 652. December 1892. 9 illustrations.

Image 5/9. "Have you found them?" She panted."
Ref. SH-SP109

Sidney Paget – The Adventure of Silver Blaze. The Strand Magazine Page 654. December 1892. 9 illustrations.

Image 6/9. "Be off!"
Ref. SH-SP110

Sidney Paget – The Adventure of Silver Blaze. The Strand Magazine Page 656. December 1892. 9 illustrations.

Image 7/9. “Holmes was extremely pleased.”
Ref. SH-SP111

Sidney Paget – The Adventure of Silver Blaze. The Strand Magazine Page 658. December 1892. 9 illustrations.

Image 8/9. "He laid his hand upon the glossy neck."
Ref. SH-SP112

Sidney Paget – The Adventure of Silver Blaze. The Strand Magazine Page 660. December 1892. 9 illustrations.

Image 9/9. “Silver Blaze.”
Ref. SH-SP113

Sidney Paget – The Adventure of the Cardboard Box. The Strand Magazine Page 61. January 1893. 8 illustrations.

Image 1/8. “I fell into a brown study.”
Ref. SH-SP114

Sidney Paget – The Adventure of the Cardboard Box. The Strand Magazine Page 63. January 1893. 8 illustrations.

Image 2/8. “Miss Cushing.”
Ref. SH-SP115

Sidney Paget – The Adventure of the Cardboard Box. The Strand Magazine Page 64. January 1893. 8 illustrations.

Image 3/8. "He examined them minutely."
Ref. SH-SP116

Sidney Paget – The Adventure of the Cardboard Box. The Strand Magazine Page 66. January 1893. 8 illustrations.

Image 4/8. "How far to Wallington?"
Ref. SH-SP117

Sidney Paget – The Adventure of the Cardboard Box. The Strand Magazine Page 68. January 1893. 8 illustrations.

Image 5/8. "Jim Browner."
Ref. SH-SP118

Sidney Paget – The Adventure of the Cardboard Box. The Strand Magazine Page 70. January 1893. 8 illustrations.

Image 6/8. "He held out his hands quietly."
Ref. SH-SP119

Sidney Paget – The Adventure of the Cardboard Box. The Strand Magazine Page 71. January 1893. 8 illustrations.

Image 7/8. " 'That's all right, my lass,.' Said I"
Ref. SH-SP120

Sidney Paget – The Adventure of the Cardboard Box. The Strand Magazine Page 73. January 1893. 8 illustrations.

Image 8/8. I got one in with my stick, that crushed his head like an egg.
Ref. SH-SP121

Sidney Paget – The Adventure of the Yellow Face. The Strand Magazine Page 163. February 1893. 7 illustrations.

Image 1/7. "He held it up."
Ref. SH-SP122

Sidney Paget – The Adventure of the Yellow Face. The Strand Magazine Page 164. February 1893. 7 illustrations.

Image 2/7. "Our visitor sprang from his chair."
Ref. SH-SP123

Sidney Paget – The Adventure of the Yellow Face. The Strand Magazine Page 166. February 1893. 7 illustrations.

Image 3/7. "What may you be wantin'?"
Ref. SH-SP124

Sidney Paget – The Adventure of the Yellow Face. The Strand Magazine Page 167. February 1893. 7 illustrations.

Image 4/7. " 'Trust me, Jack!' she cried."
Ref. SH-SP125

Sidney Paget – The Adventure of the Yellow Face. The Strand Magazine Page 169. February 1893. 7 illustrations.

Image 5/7. " 'Tell me everything,' said I."
Ref. SH-SP126

Sidney Paget – The Adventure of the Yellow Face. The Strand Magazine Page 171. February 1893. 7 illustrations.

Image 6/7. "There was a little coal-black negress."
Ref. SH-SP127

Sidney Paget – The Adventure of the Yellow Face. The Strand Magazine Page 172. February 1893. 7 illustrations.

Image 7/7. "He lifted the little child."
Ref. SH-SP128

Sidney Paget – The Adventure of the Stockbroker's Clerk. The Strand Magazine Page 281. March 1893. 7 illustrations.

Image 1/7. " 'Nothing could be better,' said Holmes."
Ref. SH-SP129

Sidney Paget – The Adventure of the Stockbroker's Clerk. The Strand Magazine Page 283. March 1893. 7 illustrations.

Image 2/7. " 'Mr. Hall Pycroft, I believe?' said he."
Ref. SH-SP130

Sidney Paget – The Adventure of the Stockbroker's Clerk. The Strand Magazine Page 285. March 1893. 7 illustrations.

Image 3/7. "Up came a man and addressed me."
Ref. SH-SP131

Sidney Paget – The Adventure of the Stockbroker's Clerk. The Strand Magazine Page 287. March 1893. 7 illustrations.

Image 4/7. "He looked at us."
Ref. SH-SP132

Sidney Paget – The Adventure of the Stockbroker's Clerk. The Strand Magazine Page 288. March 1893. 7 illustrations.

Image 5/7. "We found ourselves in the inner room."
Ref. SH-SP133

Sidney Paget – The Adventure of the Stockbroker's Clerk. The Strand Magazine Page 290. March 1893. 7 illustrations.

Image 6/7. "Pycroft shook his clenched hands in the air."
Ref. SH-SP134

Sidney Paget – The Adventure of the Stockbroker's Clerk. The Strand Magazine Page 291. March 1893. 7 illustrations.

Image 7/7. "Glancing at the haggard figure."
Ref. SH-SP135

Sidney Paget – The Adventure of the 'Gloria Scott'. The Strand Magazine Page 396. April 1893. 7 illustrations.

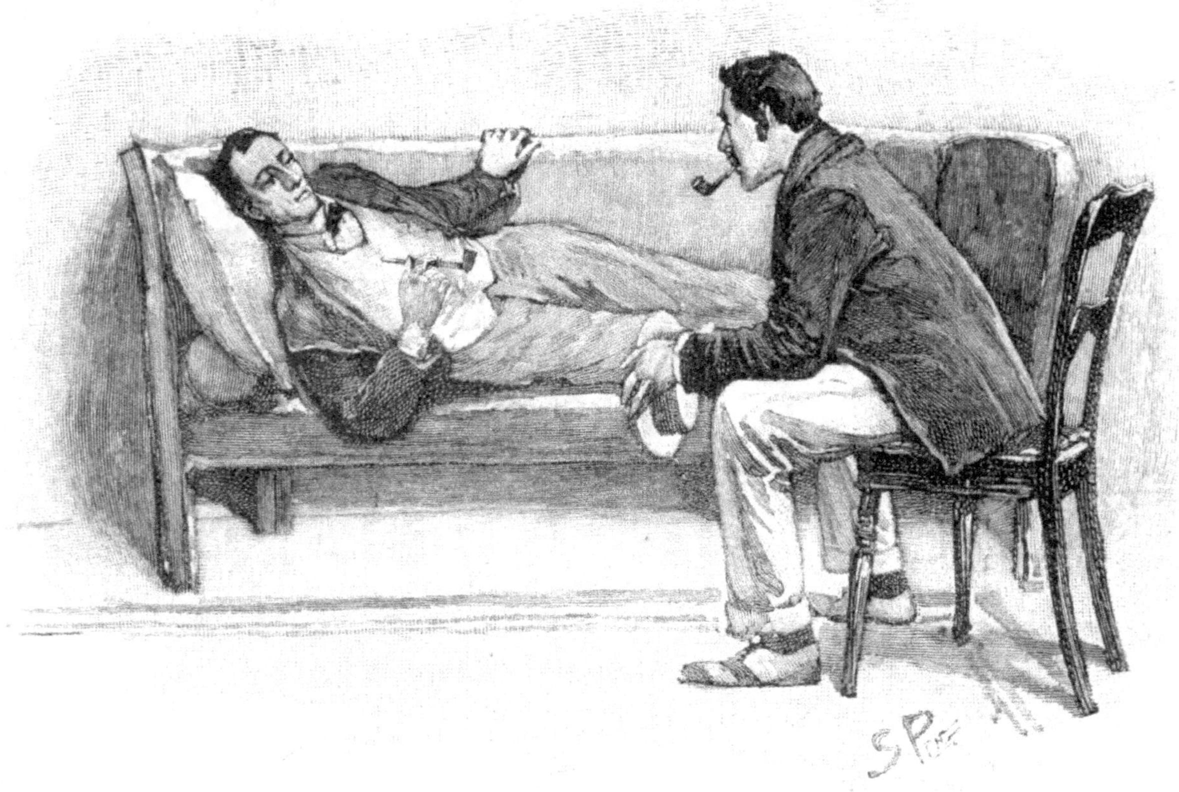

Image 1/7. "Trevor used to come in to inquire after me."
Ref. SH-SP136

Sidney Paget – The Adventure of the 'Gloria Scott'. The Strand Magazine Page 398. April 1893. 7 illustrations.

Image 2/7. " 'Hudson it is, sir,' said the seaman."
Ref. SH-SP137

Sidney Paget – The Adventure of the 'Gloria Scott'. The Strand Magazine Page 399. April 1893. 7 illustrations.

Image 3/7. " 'I've no had my 'pology,' said he, sulkily."
Ref. SH-SP138

Sidney Paget – The Adventure of the 'Gloria Scott.' The Strand Magazine Page 401. April 1893. 7 illustrations.

Image 4/7. "The key of the riddle was in my hands."
Ref. SH-SP139

Sidney Paget – The Adventure of the 'Gloria Scott'. The Strand Magazine Page 403. April 1893. 7 illustrations.

Image 5/7. "Jack Prendergast."
Ref. SH-SP140

Sidney Paget – The Adventure of the 'Gloria Scott'. The Strand Magazine Page 404. April 1893. 7 illustrations.

Image 6/7. "The Chaplain stood with a smoking pistol in his hand."
Ref. SH-SP141

Sidney Paget – The Adventure of the 'Gloria Scott'. The Strand Magazine Page 405. April 1893. 7 illustrations.

Image 7/7. "We pulled him aboard the boat."
Ref. SH-SP142

Sidney Paget – The Adventure of the Musgrave Ritual. The Strand Magazine Page 480. May 1893. 6 illustrations.

Image 1/6. “A curious collection.”
Ref. SH-SP143

Sidney Paget – The Adventure of the Musgrave Ritual. The Strand Magazine Page 481. May 1893. 6 illustrations.

Image 2/6. "Reginald Musgrave."
Ref. SH-SP144

Sidney Paget – The Adventure of the Musgrave Ritual. The Strand Magazine Page 483. May 1893. 6 illustrations.

Image 3/6. "He sprang to his feet."
Ref. SH-SP145

Sidney Paget – The Adventure of the Musgrave Ritual. The Strand Magazine Page 485. May 1893. 6 illustrations.

Image 4/6. "It has a girth of twenty-three feet."
Ref. SH-SP146

Sidney Paget – The Adventure of the Musgrave Ritual. The Strand Magazine Page 487. May 1893. 6 illustrations.

Image 5/6. "This was the place indicated."
Ref. SH-SP147

Sidney Paget – The Adventure of the Musgrave Ritual. The Strand Magazine Page 488. May 1893. 6 illustrations.

Image 6/6. “It was the figure of a man.”
Ref. SH-SP148

Sidney Paget – The Adventure of the Reigate Squires. The Strand Magazine Page 602. June 1893. 9 illustrations.

Image 1/9. "I held up a warning finger."
Ref. SH-SP149

Sidney Paget – The Adventure of the Reigate Squires. The Strand Magazine Page 603. June 1893. 9 illustrations.

Image 2/9. "Inspector Forrester."
Ref. SH-SP150

Sidney Paget – The Adventure of the Reigate Squires. The Strand Magazine Page 604. June 1893. 9 illustrations.

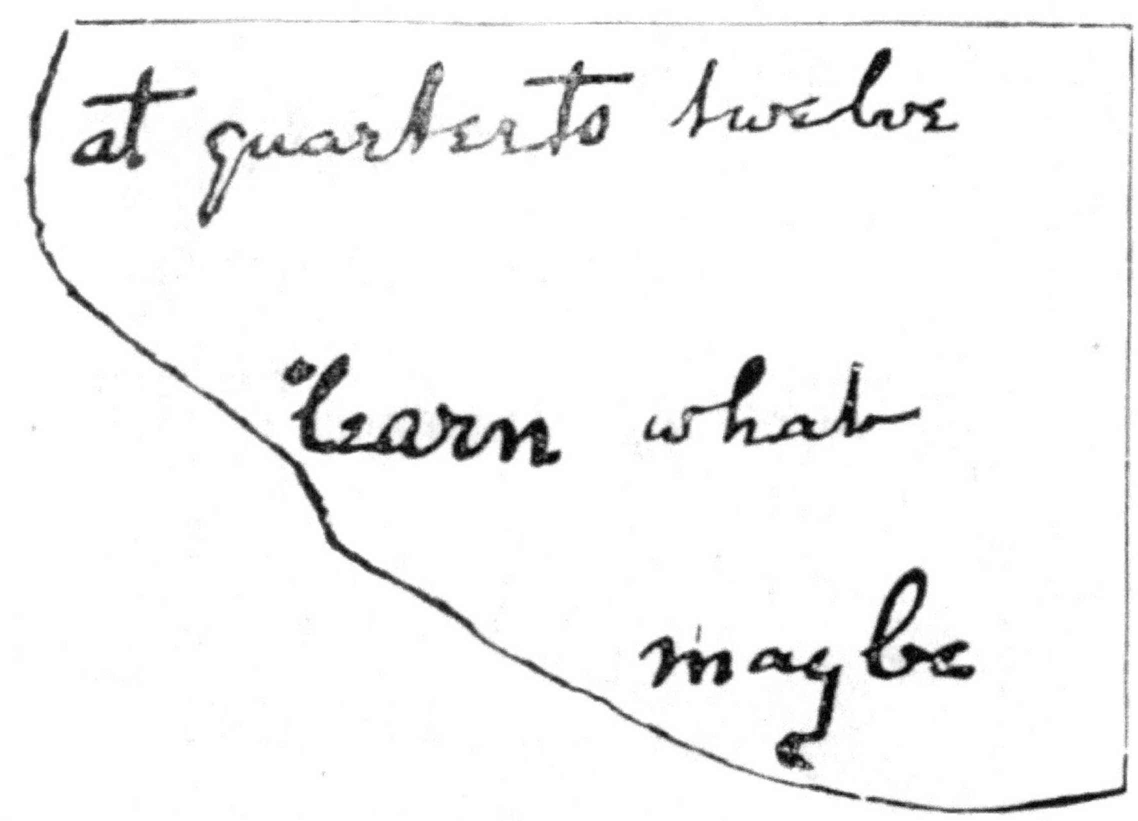
at quarter to twelve
learn what
maybe

Image 3/9. “At quarter to twelve learn what maybe”

Sidney Paget – The Adventure of the Reigate Squires. The Strand Magazine Page 606. June 1893. 9 illustrations.

Image 4/9. "Good heavens! What is the matter?"
Ref. SH-SP151

Sidney Paget – The Adventure of the Reigate Squires. The Strand Magazine Page 607. June 1893. 9 illustrations.

Image 5/9. “He deliberately knocked the whole thing over.”
Ref. SH-SP152

Sidney Paget – The Adventure of the Reigate Squires. The Strand Magazine Page 608. June 1893. 9 illustrations.

Image 6/9. "Bending over the prostrate figure of Sherlock Holmes."
Ref. SH-SP153

Sidney Paget – The Adventure of the Reigate Squires. The Strand Magazine Page 609. June 1893. 9 illustrations.

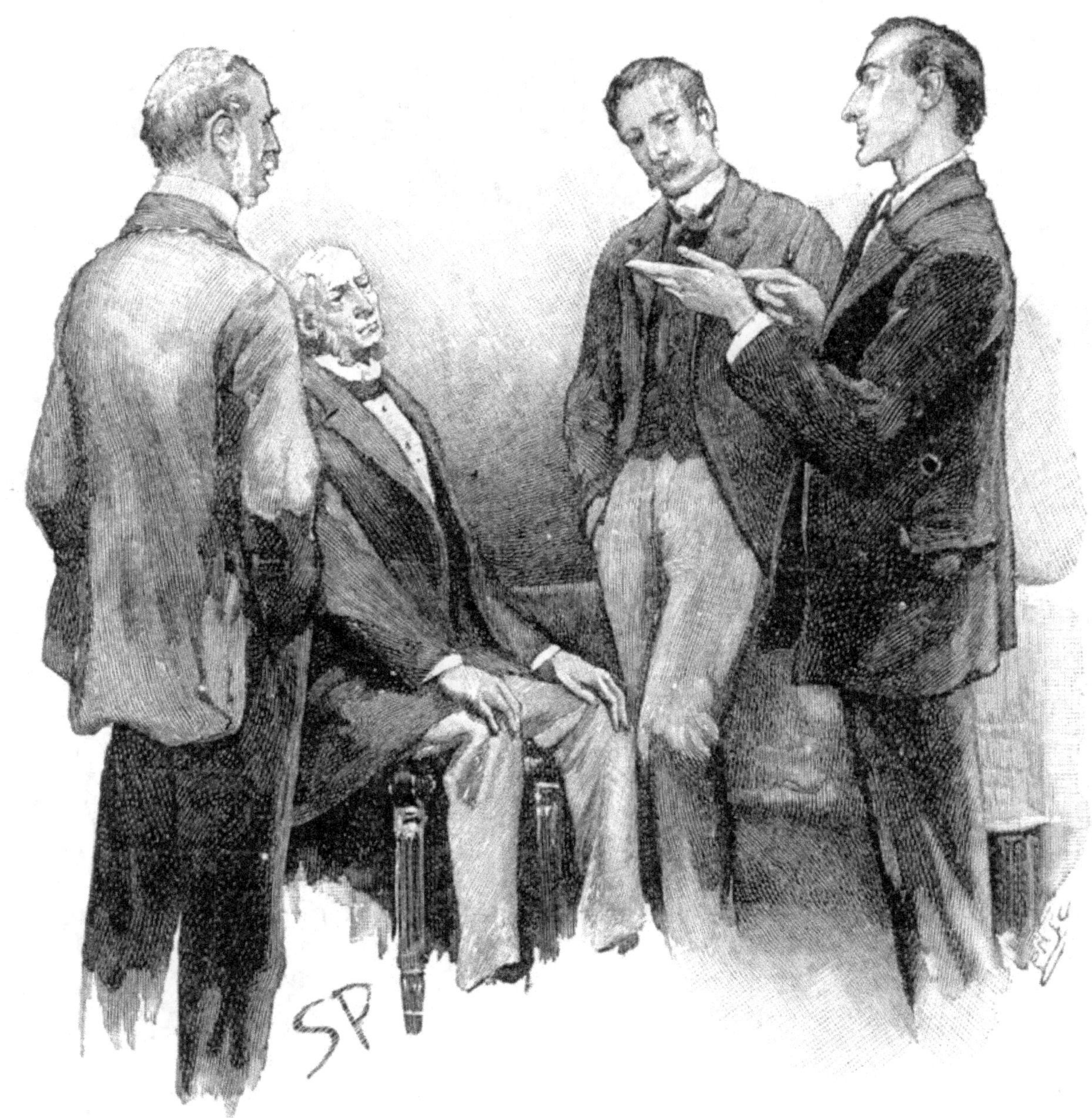

Image 7/9. “The point is a simple one.”
Ref. SH-SP154

Sidney Paget – The Adventure of the Reigate Squires. The Strand Magazine Page 611. June 1893. 9 illustrations.

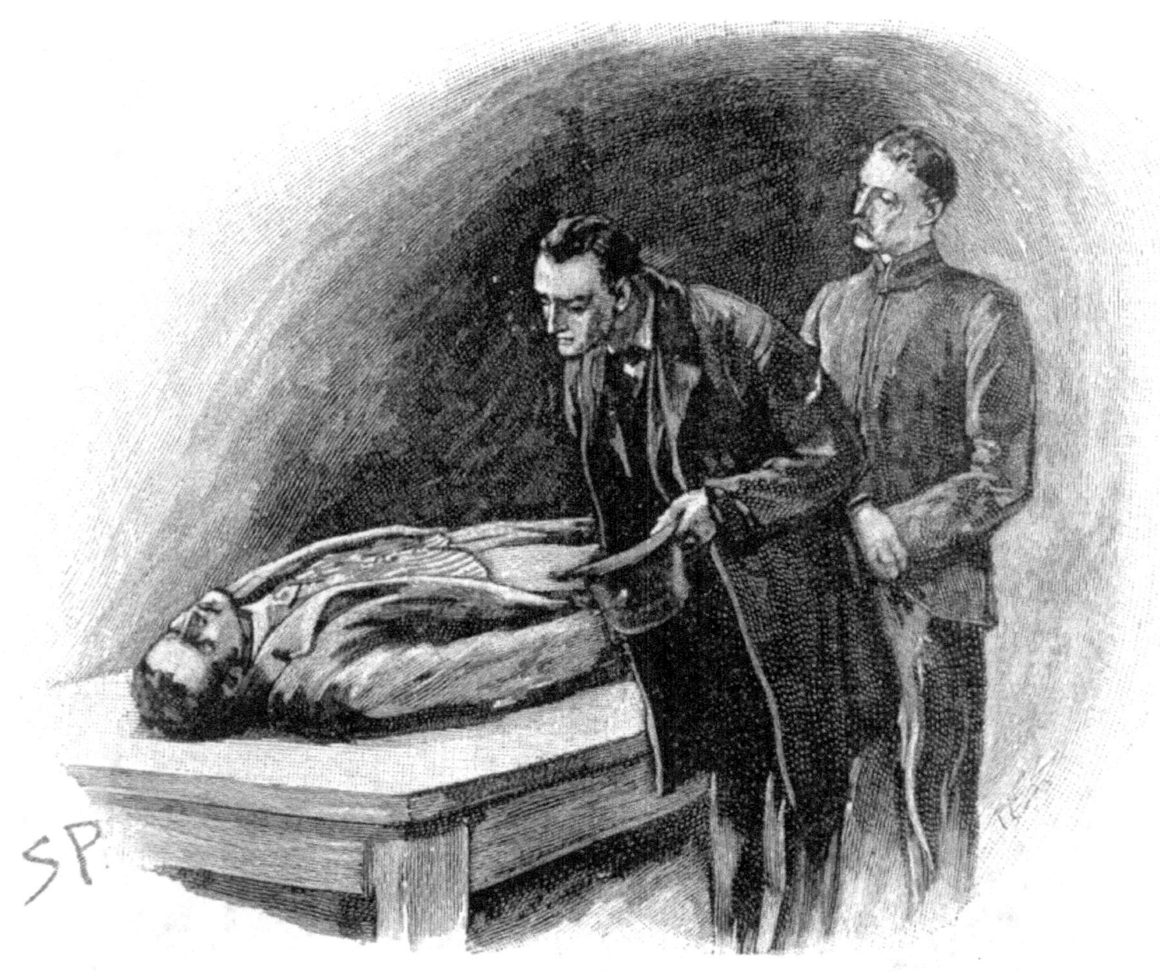

Image 8/9. "There was no powder-blackening on the clothes."
Ref. SH-SP155

Sidney Paget – The Adventure of the Reigate Squires. The Strand Magazine Page 612. June 1893. 9 illustrations.

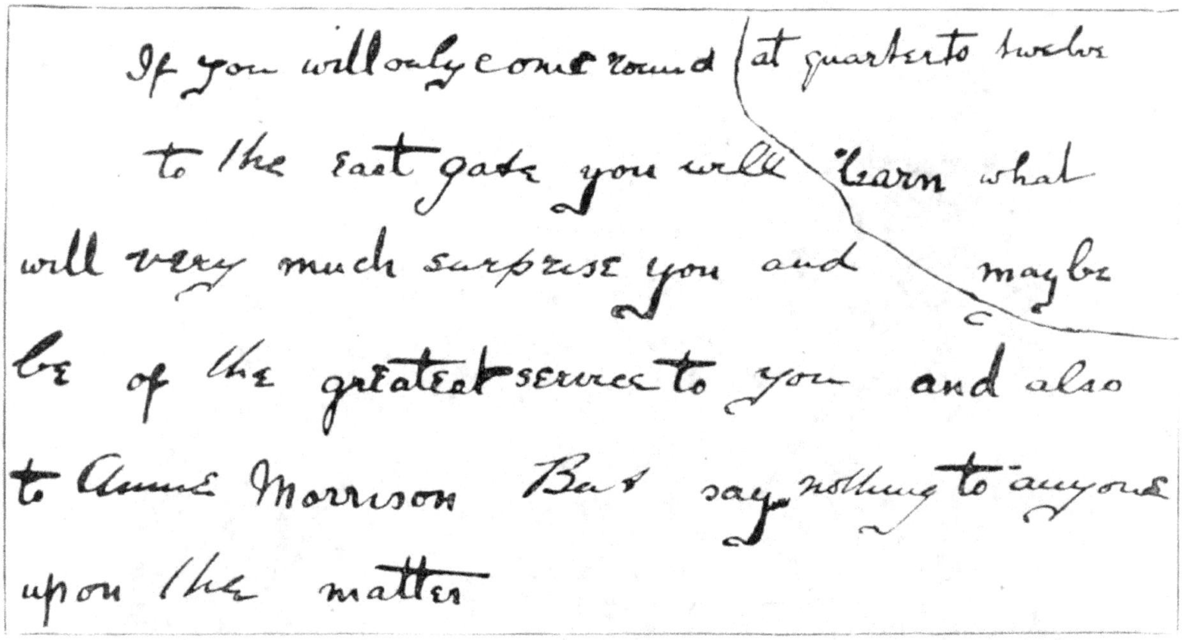

If you will only come round at quarter to twelve
to the east gate you will learn what
will very much surprise you and maybe
be of the greatest service to you and also
to Annie Morrison But say nothing to anyone
upon the matter

Image 9/9. The full note.

Sidney Paget – The Adventure of the Crooked Man. The Strand Magazine Page 22. July 1893. 7 illustrations.

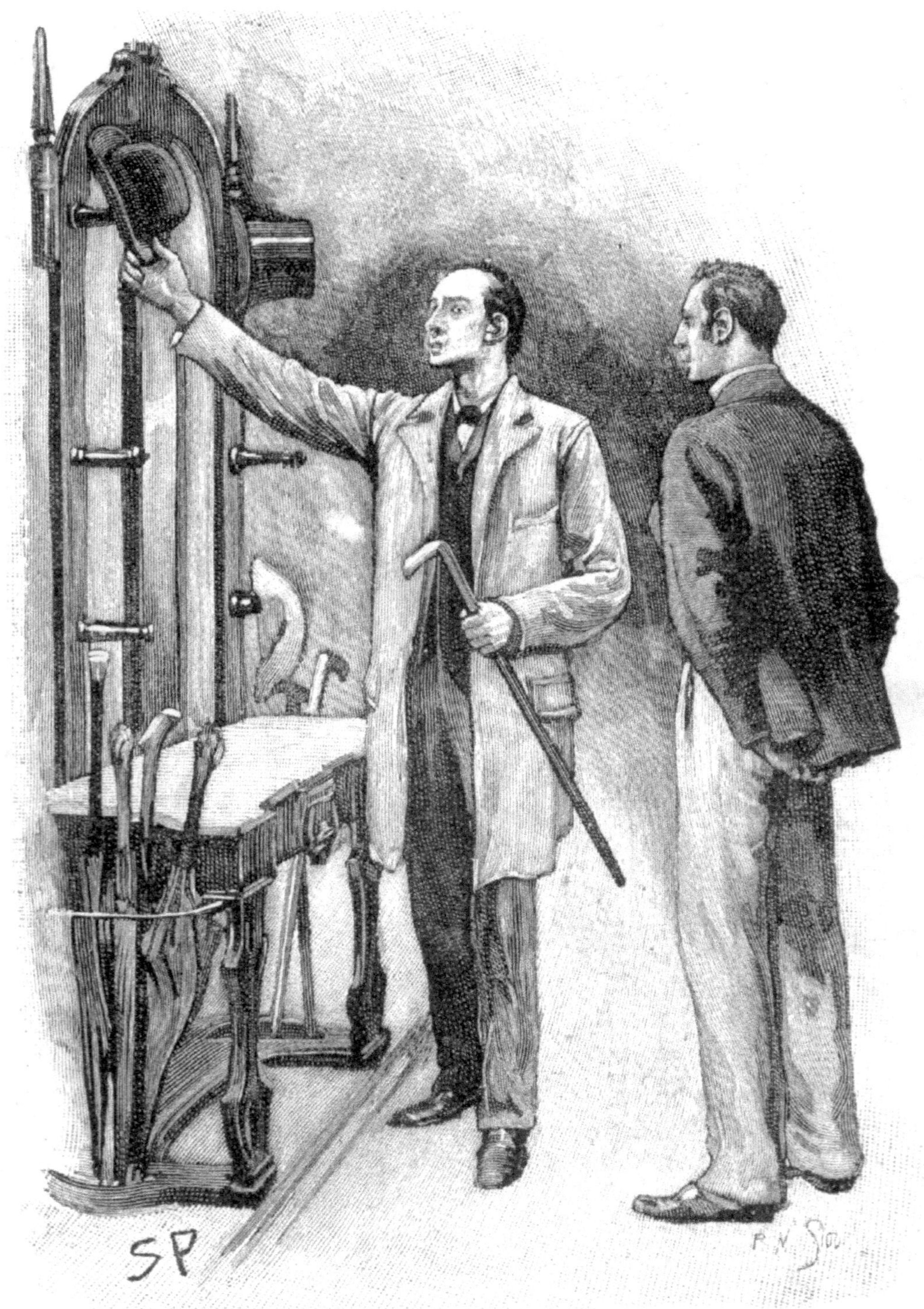

Image 1/7. “I’ll fill a vacant peg, then.”
Ref. SH-SP156

Sidney Paget – The Adventure of the Crooked Man. The Strand Magazine Page 25. July 1893. 7 illustrations.

Image 2/7. “The coachman rushed to the door.”
Ref. SH-SP157

Sidney Paget – The Adventure of the Crooked Man. The Strand Magazine Page 26. July 1893. 7 illustrations.

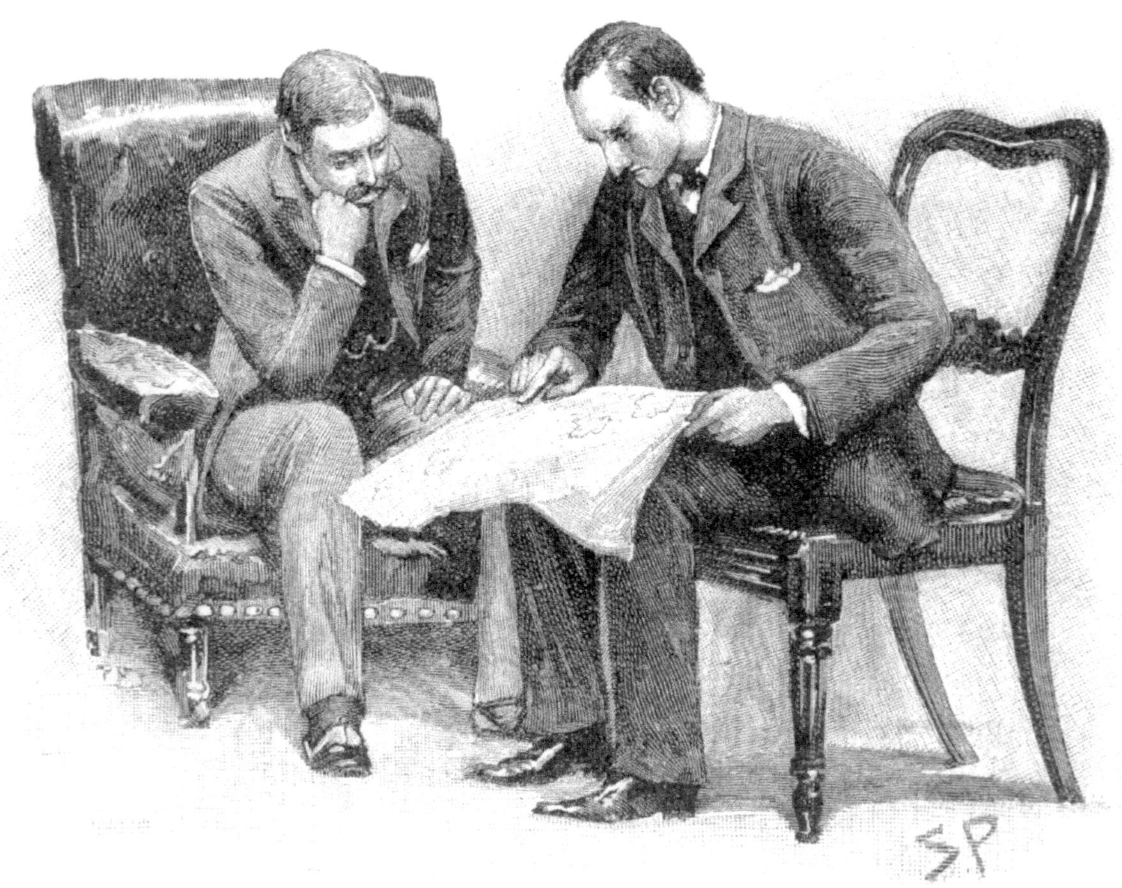

Image 3/7. "What do you make of that?"
Ref. SH-SP158

Sidney Paget – The Adventure of the Crooked Man. The Strand Magazine Page 28. July 1893. 7 illustrations.

Image 4/7. "'It's Nancy."
Ref. SH-SP159

Sidney Paget – The Adventure of the Crooked Man. The Strand Magazine Page 30. July 1893. 7 illustrations.

Image 5/7. "Mr. Henry Wood, I believe?"
Ref. SH-SP160

Sidney Paget – The Adventure of the Crooked Man. The Strand Magazine Page 31. July 1893. 7 illustrations.

Image 6/7. "I walked right into six of them."
Ref. SH-SP161

Sidney Paget – The Adventure of the Crooked Man. The Strand Magazine Page 32. July 1893. 7 illustrations.

Image 7/7. “It was quite a simple case after all.”
Ref. SH-SP162

Sidney Paget – The Adventure of the Resident Patient. The Strand Magazine Page 129. August 1893. 7 illustrations.

Image 1/7. “We strolled about together.”
Ref. SH-SP163

Sidney Paget – The Adventure of the Resident Patient. The Strand Magazine Page 130. August 1893. 7 illustrations.

Image 2/7. “I stared at him in astonishment.”
Ref. SH-SP164

Sidney Paget – The Adventure of the Resident Patient. The Strand Magazine Page 131. August 1893. 7 illustrations.

Image 3/7. "Helped him to a chair."
Ref. SH-SP165

Sidney Paget – The Adventure of the Resident Patient. The Strand Magazine Page 133. August 1893. 7 illustrations.

Image 4/7. “He burst into my consulting-room.”
Ref. SH-SP166

Sidney Paget – The Adventure of the Resident Patient. The Strand Magazine Page 134. August 1893. 7 illustrations.

Image 5/7. "In his hand he held a pistol."
Ref. SH-SP167

Sidney Paget – The Adventure of the Resident Patient. The Strand Magazine Page 136. August 1893. 7 illustrations.

Image 6/7. "Holmes opened it and smelled the single cigar which it contained."
Ref. SH-SP168

Sidney Paget – The Adventure of the Resident Patient. The Strand Magazine Page 137. August 1893. 7 illustrations.

Image 7/7. " 'You have got them!' we cried."
Ref. SH-SP169

Sidney Paget – The Adventure of the Greek Interpreter. The Strand Magazine Page 297. September 1893. 8 illustrations.

Image 1/8. “Holmes pulled out his watch.”
Ref. SH-SP170

Sidney Paget – The Adventure of the Greek Interpreter. The Strand Magazine Page 298. September 1893. 8 illustrations.

Image 2/8. Mycroft Holmes.
Ref. SH-SP171

Sidney Paget – The Adventure of the Greek Interpreter. The Strand Magazine Page 299. September 1893. 8 illustrations.

Image 3/8. "He drew up the windows."
Ref. SH-SP172

Sidney Paget – The Adventure of the Greek Interpreter. The Strand Magazine Page 301. September 1893. 8 illustrations.

Image 4/8. “I was thrilled with horror.”
Ref. SH-SP173

Sidney Paget – The Adventure of the Greek Interpreter. The Strand Magazine Page 302. September 1893. 8 illustrations.

Image 5/8. "Sophy! Sophy!"
Ref. SH-SP174

Sidney Paget – The Adventure of the Greek Interpreter. The Strand Magazine Page 303. September 1893. 8 illustrations.

Image 6/8. “I saw someone coming towards me.”
Ref. SH-SP175

Sidney Paget – The Adventure of the Greek Interpreter. The Strand Magazine Page 304. September 1893. 8 illustrations.

Image 7/8. " 'Come in,' said he, blandly"
Ref. SH-SP176

Sidney Paget – The Adventure of the Greek Interpreter. The Strand Magazine Page 306. September 1893. 8 illustrations.

Image 8/8. " 'It's charcoal,' he cried."
Ref. SH-SP177

Sidney Paget – The Adventure of the Naval Treaty (1/2). The Strand Magazine Page 393. October 1893. 9 illustrations.

Image 1/9. " Holmes was working hard over a chemical investigation."
Ref. SH-SP178

Sidney Paget – The Adventure of the Naval Treaty (1/2). The Strand Magazine Page 394. October 1893. 9 illustrations.

Image 2/9. " 'I won't waste your time,' said he."
Ref. SH-SP179

Sidney Paget – The Adventure of the Naval Treaty (1/2). The Strand Magazine Page 395. October 1893. 9 illustrations.

Image 3/9. "Then take the treaty"
Ref. SH-SP180

Sidney Paget – The Adventure of the Naval Treaty (1/2). The Strand Magazine Page 396. October 1893. 9 illustrations.

Image 4/9. “Fast asleep in his box.”
Ref. SH-SP181

Sidney Paget – The Adventure of the Naval Treaty (1/2). The Strand Magazine Page 396. October 1893. 9 illustrations.

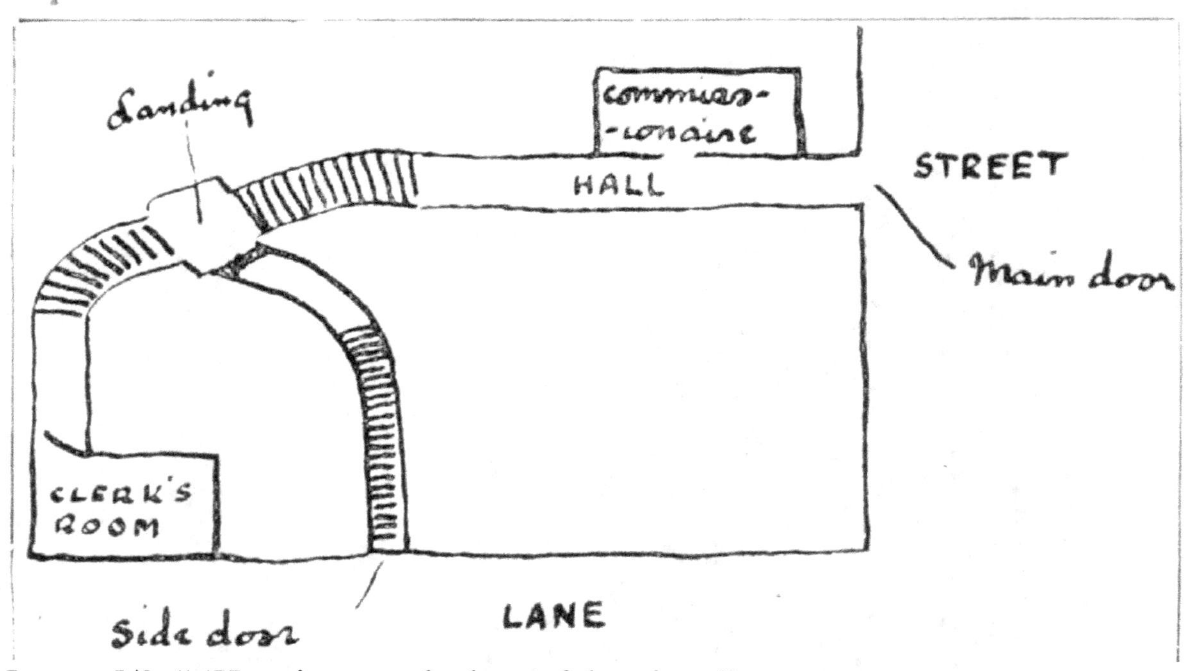

Image 5/9. " 'Here is a rough chart of the place."

Sidney Paget – The Adventure of the Naval Treaty (1/2). The Strand Magazine Page 398. October 1893. 9 illustrations.

Image 6/9. "Why, if it isn't Mr. Phelps!"
Ref. SH-SP182

Sidney Paget – The Adventure of the Naval Treaty (1/2). The Strand Magazine Page 400. October 1893. 9 illustrations.

Image 7/9. "What a lovely thing a rose is."
Ref. SH-SP183

Sidney Paget – The Adventure of the Naval Treaty (1/2). The Strand Magazine Page 297. October 1893. 9 illustrations.

Image 8/9. "The view was sordid enough."
Ref. SH-SP184

Sidney Paget – The Adventure of the Naval Treaty (1/2). The Strand Magazine Page 402. October 1893. 9 illustrations.

Image 9/9. "I've heard of your methods before now, Mr. Holmes."
Ref. SH-SP185

Sidney Paget – The Adventure of the Naval Treaty (2/2). The Strand Magazine Page 459. November 1893. 7 illustrations.

Image 1/7. “A nobleman.”
Ref. SH-SP186

Sidney Paget – The Adventure of the Naval Treaty (2/2). The Strand Magazine Page 461. November 1893. 7 illustrations.

Image 2/7. " 'Any news?' he asked."
Ref. SH-SP187

Sidney Paget – The Adventure of the Naval Treaty (2/2). The Strand Magazine Page 462. November 1893. 7 illustrations.

Image 3/7. "Holmes examined it critically."
Ref. SH-SP188

Sidney Paget – The Adventure of the Naval Treaty (2/2). The Strand Magazine Page 463. November 1893. 7 illustrations.

Image 4/7. "I hardly expect to go back to Briarbrae."
Ref. SH-SP189

Sidney Paget – The Adventure of the Naval Treaty (2/2). The Strand Magazine Page 465. November 1893. 7 illustrations.

Image 5/7. "Phelps raised the cover."
Ref. SH-SP190

Sidney Paget – The Adventure of the Naval Treaty (2/2). The Strand Magazine Page 466. November 1893. 7 illustrations.

Image 6/7. " Joseph Harrison stepped out."
Ref. SH-SP191

Sidney Paget – The Adventure of the Naval Treaty (2/2). The Strand Magazine Page 468. November 1893. 7 illustrations.

Image 7/7. Is there any other point which I can make clear?
Ref. SH-SP192

Sidney Paget – The Adventure of the Final Problem. The Strand Magazine Page 558. December 1893. 9 illustrations.

Image 1/9. The death of Sherlock Holmes.
Ref. SH-SP193

Sidney Paget – The Adventure of the Final Problem. The Strand Magazine Page 560. December 1893. 9 illustrations.

Image 2/9. "Two of his knuckles were burst and bleeding."
Ref. SH-SP194

Sidney Paget – The Adventure of the Final Problem. The Strand Magazine Page 561. December 1893. 9 illustrations.

Image 3/9. " Professor Moriarty stood before me."
Ref. SH-SP195

Sidney Paget – The Adventure of the Final Problem. The Strand Magazine Page 563. December 1893. 9 illustrations.

Image 4/9. "He turned his rounded back upon me."
Ref. SH-SP196

Sidney Paget – The Adventure of the Final Problem. The Strand Magazine Page 565. December 1893. 9 illustrations.

Image 5/8. My decrepit Italian friend."
Ref. SH-SP197

Sidney Paget – The Adventure of the Final Problem. The Strand Magazine Page 566. December 1893. 9 illustrations.

Image 6/9. “It passed with a rattle and a roar.”
Ref. SH-SP198

Sidney Paget – The Adventure of the Final Problem. The Strand Magazine Page 567. December 1893. 9 illustrations.

Image 7/9. "A large rock clattered down."
Ref. SH-SP199

Sidney Paget – The Adventure of the Final Problem. The Strand Magazine Page 568. December 1893. 9 illustrations.

Image 8/9. " I saw Holmes gazing down at the rush of the waters."
Ref. SH-SP200

Sidney Paget – The Adventure of the Final Problem. The Strand Magazine Page 570. December 1893. 9 illustrations.

Image 9/9. "A small square of paper fluttered down."
Ref. SH-SP201

Sidney Paget – The Hound of the Baskervilles (1/9). The Strand Magazine Page 122. August 1901. 7 illustrations.

Image 1/7. “The Hound of the Baskervilles” *(See page 128.)*
Ref. SH-SP202

Sidney Paget – The Hound of the Baskervilles (1/9). The Strand Magazine Page 124. August 1901. 7 illustrations.

Image 2/7. "He looked over it again with a convex lens."
Ref. SH-SP203

Sidney Paget – The Hound of the Baskervilles (1/9). The Strand Magazine Page 125. August 1901. 7 illustrations.

Image 3/7. "His eyes fell upon the stick in Holmes's hand."
Ref. SH-SP204

Sidney Paget – The Hound of the Baskervilles (1/9). The Strand Magazine Page 127. August 1901. 7 illustrations.

Image 4/7. "Dr. Mortimer turned the manuscript to the light and read."
Ref. SH-SP205

Sidney Paget – The Hound of the Baskervilles (1/9). The Strand Magazine Page 129. August 1901. 7 illustrations.

Image 5/7. "There in the centre lay the unhappy maid where she had fallen."
Ref. SH-SP206

Sidney Paget – The Hound of the Baskervilles (1/9). The Strand Magazine Page 130. August 1901. 7 illustrations.

Image 6/7. "His body was discovered."
Ref. SH-SP207

Sidney Paget – The Hound of the Baskervilles (1/9). The Strand Magazine Page 132. August 1901. 7 illustrations.

Image 7/7. "I saw his eyes fix themselves over my shoulder."
Ref. SH-SP208

Sidney Paget – The Hound of the Baskervilles (2/9). The Strand Magazine Page 242. September 1901. 8 illustrations.

Image 1/8. "There's our man, Watson! Come along."

Ref. SH-SP209

(See page 253.)

Sidney Paget – The Hound of the Baskervilles (2/9). The Strand Magazine Page 224. September 1901. 8 illustrations.

Image 2/8. "You have indeed much to answer for."
Ref. SH-SP210

Sidney Paget – The Hound of the Baskervilles (2/9). The Strand Magazine Page 246. September 1901. 8 illustrations.

Image 3/8. "He scribbled the appointment on his shirt cuff."
Ref. SH-SP211

Sidney Paget – The Hound of the Baskervilles (2/9). The Strand Magazine Page 247. September 1901. 8 illustrations.

Image 4/8. "That is Baskerville Hall in the middle."
Ref. SH-SP212

Sidney Paget – The Hound of the Baskervilles (2/9). The Strand Magazine Page 248. September 1901. 8 illustrations.

Image 5/8. "Sir Henry Baskerville."
Ref. SH-SP213

Sidney Paget – The Hound of the Baskervilles (2/9). The Strand Magazine Page 249. September 1901. 8 illustrations.

Image 6/8. "He glanced swiftly over it."
Ref. SH-SP214

Sidney Paget – The Hound of the Baskervilles (2/9). The Strand Magazine Page 251. September 1901. 8 illustrations.

Image 7/8. "Holding it only an inch or two from his eyes."
Ref. SH-SP215

Sidney Paget – The Hound of the Baskervilles (2/9). The Strand Magazine Page 253. September 1901. 8 illustrations.

Image 8/8. “Here are the names of twenty-three hotels.”
Ref. SH-SP216

Sidney Paget – The Hound of the Baskervilles (3/9). The Strand Magazine Page 362. October 1903. 7 illustrations.

Image 1/7. "The driver pointed with his whip- 'Baskerville Hall,' said he."
Ref. SH-SP217

(See page 371.)

Sidney Paget – The Hound of the Baskervilles (3/9). The Strand Magazine Page 364. October 1901. 7 illustrations.

Image 2/7. "He held an old and dusty boot in one of his hands."
Ref. SH-SP218

Sidney Paget – The Hound of the Baskervilles (3/9). The Strand Magazine Page 366. October 1901. 7 illustrations.

Image 3/7. "The proposition took me completely by surprise."
Ref. SH-SP219

Sidney Paget – The Hound of the Baskervilles (3/9). The Strand Magazine Page 367. October 1901. 7 illustrations.

Image 4/7. " 'His name,' said the cabman, 'was Mr. Sherlock Holmes.' "
Ref. SH-SP220

Sidney Paget – The Hound of the Baskervilles (3/9). The Strand Magazine Page 369. October 1901. 7 illustrations.

Image 5/7. "Our friends were waiting for us upon the platform."
Ref. SH-SP221

Sidney Paget – The Hound of the Baskervilles (3/9). The Strand Magazine Page 371. October 1901. 7 illustrations.

Image 6/7. "Welcome, Sir Henry!"
Ref. SH-SP222

Sidney Paget – The Hound of the Baskervilles (3/9). The Strand Magazine Page 373. October 1901. 7 illustrations.

Image 7/7. "The dining-room was a place of shadow and gloom."
Ref. SH-SP223

Sidney Paget – The Hound of the Baskervilles (4/9). The Strand Magazine Page 496. November 1901. 7 illustrations.

Image 1/7. "It was a stranger pursuing me."
Ref. SH-SP224

Sidney Paget – The Hound of the Baskervilles (4/9). The Strand Magazine Page 498. November 1901. 7 illustrations.

Image 2/7. "That is the great Grimpen Mire"
Ref. SH-SP225

Sidney Paget – The Hound of the Baskervilles (4/9). The Strand Magazine Page 500. November 1901. 7 illustrations.

Image 3/7. " 'Go back!' she said."
Ref. SH-SP226

Sidney Paget – The Hound of the Baskervilles (4/9). The Strand Magazine Page 502. November 1901. 7 illustrations.

Image 4/7. "You know the story of the hound?"
Ref. SH-SP227

Sidney Paget – The Hound of the Baskervilles (4/9). The Strand Magazine Page 503. November 1901. 7 illustrations.

Image 5/7. “He took us to show us the spot.”
Ref. SH-SP228

Sidney Paget – The Hound of the Baskervilles (4/9). The Strand Magazine Page 504. November 1901. 7 illustrations.

Image 6/7. “The yew alley.”
Ref. SH-SP229

Sidney Paget – The Hound of the Baskervilles (4/9). The Strand Magazine Page 506. November 1901. 7 illustrations.

Image 7/7. "He stared out into the blackness."
Ref. SH-SP230

Sidney Paget – The Hound of the Baskervilles (1/6). The Strand Magazine Page 602. December 1901. 6 illustrations.

Image 1/6. "Over the rocks was thrust out an evil yellow face."

Ref. SH-SP231

(See page 611.)

Sidney Paget – The Hound of the Baskervilles (2/6). The Strand Magazine Page 604. December 1901. 6 illustrations.

Image 2/6. “Sir Henry put his hand upon my shoulder.”
Ref. SH-SP232

Sidney Paget – The Hound of the Baskervilles (3/6). The Strand Magazine Page 606. December 1901. 6 illustrations.

Image 3/6. “Sir Henry suddenly drew Miss Stapleton to his side.”
Ref. SH-SP233

Sidney Paget – The Hound of the Baskervilles (4/6). The Strand Magazine Page 608. December 1901. 6 illustrations.

Image 4/6. "What are you doing here, Barrymore?"
Ref. SH-SP234

Sidney Paget – The Hound of the Baskervilles (5/6). The Strand Magazine Page 609. December 1901. 6 illustrations.

Image 5/6. "The escaped convict, Sir"
Ref. SH-SP235

Sidney Paget – The Hound of the Baskervilles (5/9). The Strand Magazine Page 611. December 1901. 6 illustrations.

Image 6/6. "I saw the figure of a man upon the tor."
Ref. SH-SP236

Sidney Paget – The Hound of the Baskervilles (6/9). The Strand Magazine Page 1. January 1902. 7 illustrations.

Image 1/7. “The shadow of Sherlock Holmes.”
Ref. SH-SP237

(See page 15.)

Sidney Paget – The Hound of the Baskervilles (6/9). The Strand Magazine Page 4. January 1902. 7 illustrations.

Image 2/7. "The butler was standing, very pale but very collected, before us."
Ref. SH-SP238

Sidney Paget – The Hound of the Baskervilles (6/9). The Strand Magazine Page 6. January 1902. 7 illustrations.

Image 3/7. "From its craggy summit I looked out myself across the melancholy downs."
Ref. SH-SP239

Sidney Paget – The Hound of the Baskervilles (6/9). The Strand Magazine Page 8. January 1902. 7 illustrations.

Image 4/7. "You know that there is another man, then?"
Ref. SH-SP240

Sidney Paget – The Hound of the Baskervilles (6/9). The Strand Magazine Page 10. January 1902. 7 illustrations.

Image 5/7. "Really, sir, this is a very extraordinary question."
Ref. SH-SP241

Sidney Paget – The Hound of the Baskervilles (6/9). The Strand Magazine Page 12. January 1902. 7 illustrations.

Image 6/7. " 'Good-day, Dr. Watson,' he cried."
Ref. SH-SP242

Sidney Paget – The Hound of the Baskervilles (6/9). The Strand Magazine Page 14. January 1902. 7 illustrations.

Image 7/7. "Frankland clapped his eye to it and gave a cry of satisfaction."
Ref. SH-SP243

Sidney Paget – The Hound of the Baskervilles (7/9). The Strand Magazine Page 122. February 1902. 4 illustrations.

Image 1/4. "It was a prostrate man face downwards upon the ground."
Ref. SH-SP244

(See page 126.)

Sidney Paget – The Hound of the Baskervilles (7/9). The Strand Magazine Page 124. February 1902. 4 illustrations.

Image 2/4. "There he sat upon a stone."
Ref. SH-SP245

Sidney Paget – The Hound of the Baskervilles (7/9). The Strand Magazine Page 127. February 1902. 4 illustrations.

Image 3/4. "It was the face of Selden the criminal."
Ref. SH-SP246

Sidney Paget – The Hound of the Baskervilles (7/9). The Strand Magazine Page 129. February 1902. 4 illustrations.

Image 4/4. " 'Who – Who's this?' he stammered."
Ref. SH-SP247

Sidney Paget – The Hound of the Baskervilles (8/9). The Strand Magazine Page 242. March 1902. 7 illustrations.

Image 1/7. "The Hound of the Baskervilles."
Ref. SH-SP248

(See page 252.)

Sidney Paget – The Hound of the Baskervilles (8/9). The Strand Magazine Page 244. March 1902. 7 illustrations.

Image 2/7. "He stopped suddenly and stared fixedly up over my head into the air."
Ref. SH-SP249

Sidney Paget – The Hound of the Baskervilles (8/9). The Strand Magazine Page 245. March 1902. 7 illustrations.

Image 3/7. " 'Good Heavens!' I cried, in amazement."
Ref. SH-SP250

Sidney Paget – The Hound of the Baskervilles (8/9). The Strand Magazine Page 247. March 1902. 7 illustrations.

Image 4/7. "The lady sprang from her chair."
Ref. SH-SP251

Sidney Paget – The Hound of the Baskervilles (8/9). The Strand Magazine Page 249. March 1902. 7 illustrations.

Image 5/7. "We all three shook hands."
Ref. SH-SP252

Sidney Paget – The Hound of the Baskervilles (8/9). The Strand Magazine Page 250. March 1902. 7 illustrations.

Image 6/7. "I could look straight through the uncurtained windows."
Ref. SH-SP253

Sidney Paget – The Hound of the Baskervilles (8/9). The Strand Magazine Page 252. March 1902. 7 illustrations.

Image 7/7. "He looked round him in surprise."
Ref. SH-SP254

Sidney Paget – The Hound of the Baskervilles (9/9). The Strand Magazine Page 362. April 1902. 7 illustrations.

Image 1/7. "Holmes emptied five barrels of his revolver into the creature's flank."
Ref. SH-SP255

(See page 363.)

Sidney Paget – The Hound of the Baskervilles (9/9). The Strand Magazine Page 364. April 1902. 7 illustrations.

Image 2/7. " 'Phosphorus!' I said."
Ref. SH-SP256

Sidney Paget – The Hound of the Baskervilles (9/9). The Strand Magazine Page 365. April 1902. 7 illustrations.

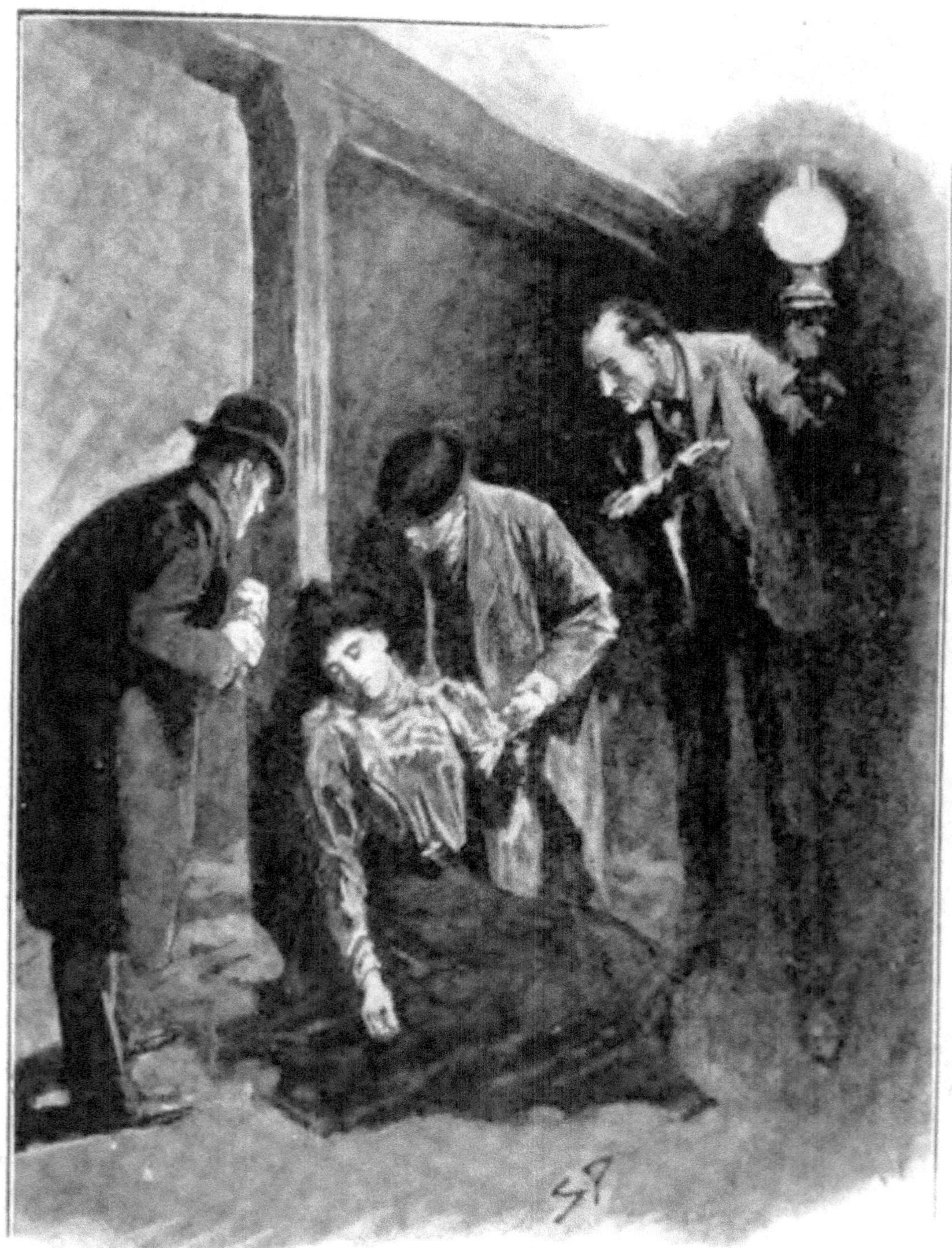

Image 3/7. "Mrs. Stapleton sank upon the floor."
Ref. SH-SP257

Sidney Paget – The Hound of the Baskervilles (9/9). The Strand Magazine Page 366. April 1902. 7 illustrations.

Image 4/7. "He held an old black boot in the air."
Ref. SH-SP258

Sidney Paget – The Hound of the Baskervilles (9/9). The Strand Magazine Page 367. April 1902. 7 illustrations.

Image 5/7. "Where the animal had been confined."
Ref. SH-SP259

Sidney Paget – The Hound of the Baskervilles (9/9). The Strand Magazine Page 368. April 1902. 7 illustrations.

Image 6/7. "A retrospection."
Ref. SH-SP260

Sidney Paget – The Hound of the Baskervilles (9/9). The Strand Magazine Page 371. April 1902. 7 illustrations.

Image 7/7. “Be ready in half an hour.”
Ref. SH-SP261

Sidney Paget – The Adventure of the Empty House. The Strand Magazine Page 362. October 1903. 7 illustrations.

Image 1/7. "He seized Holmes by the throat."
Ref. SH-SP262

(See page 372.)

Sidney Paget – The Adventure of the Empty House. The Strand Magazine Page 365. October 1903. 7 illustrations.

Image 2/7. “I knocked down several books which he was carrying.”
Ref. SH-SP263

Sidney Paget – The Adventure of the Empty House. The Strand Magazine Page 366. October 1903. 7 illustrations.

Image 3/7. "Sherlock Holmes was standing smiling at me across my study table."
Ref. SH-SP264

Sidney Paget – The Adventure of the Empty House. The Strand Magazine Page 369. October 1903. 7 illustrations.

Image 4/7. "I crept forward and looked across at the familiar window."
Ref. SH-SP265

Sidney Paget – The Adventure of the Empty House. The Strand Magazine Page 371. October 1903. 7 illustrations.

Image 5/7. "The light of the street fell full upon his face."
Ref. SH-SP266

Sidney Paget – The Adventure of the Empty House. The Strand Magazine Page 373. October 1903. 7 illustrations.

Image 6/7. "Colonel Moran sprang forward, with a snarl of rage."
Ref. SH-SP267

Sidney Paget – The Adventure of the Empty House. The Strand Magazine Page 375. October 1903. 7 illustrations.

Image 7/7. " 'My collection of M's is a fine one,' said he."
Ref. SH-SP268

Sidney Paget – The Adventure of the Norwood Builder. The Strand Magazine Page 482. November 1903. 7 illustrations.

Image 1/7. "A little, wizened man darted out."
Ref. SH-SP269

(See page 494.)

Sidney Paget – The Adventure of the Norwood Builder. The Strand Magazine Page 484. November 1903. 7 illustrations.

Image 2/7. “A wild-eyed and frantic young man burst into the room.”
Ref. SH-SP270

Sidney Paget – The Adventure of the Norwood Builder. The Strand Magazine Page 487. November 1903. 7 illustrations.

Image 3/7. "The wretched young man arose."
Ref. SH-SP271

Sidney Paget – The Adventure of the Norwood Builder. The Strand Magazine Page 489. November 1903. 7 illustrations.

Image 4/7. "My first movement, Watson,' said he, 'must be in the direction of Blackheath."
Ref. SH-SP272

Sidney Paget – The Adventure of the Norwood Builder. The Strand Magazine Page 490. November 1903. 7 illustrations.

Image 5/7. “He sent it to me in that State, with his curse, upon my wedding morning.”
Ref. SH-SP273

Sidney Paget – The Adventure of the Norwood Builder. The Strand Magazine Page 492. November 1903. 7 illustrations.

Image 6/7. "Look at that with your magnifying glass, Mr. Holmes."
Ref. SH-SP274

Sidney Paget – The Adventure of the Norwood Builder. The Strand Magazine Page 495. November 1903. 7 illustrations.

Image 7/7. "Holmes smiled and clapped Lestrade upon the shoulder."
Ref. SH-SP275

Sidney Paget – The Adventure of the Dancing Men. The Strand Magazine Page 602. December 1903. 13 illustrations.

Image 1/13. “Holmes clapped a pistol to his head and martin slipped the handcuffs over his wrists.”
Ref. SH-SP276

(See page 616.)

Sidney Paget – The Adventure of the Dancing Men. The Strand Magazine Page 484. December 1903. 13 illustrations.

Image 2/13. "Holmes held up the paper."
Ref. SH-SP277

Sidney Paget – The Adventure of the Dancing Men. The Strand Magazine Page 604. December 1903

Image 3/13. "AM HERE ABE SLANEY."

Image 4/13. "AT ELRIGES."

Image 5/13. "COME ELSIE."

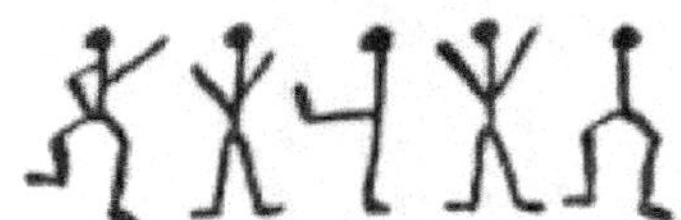

Image 6/13. "NEVER."

Image 7/13. "ELSIE PREPARE TO MEET THY GOD."

Image 8/13. "COME HERE AT ONCE."

Letter	Figure
A	
B	
C	
D	
E	
F	-
G	
H	
I	
J	-
K	-
L	
M	
N	
O	
P	
Q	-
R	
S	
T	
U	-
V	
W	-
X	-
Y	
Z	-

Sidney Paget – The Adventure of the Dancing Men. The Strand Magazine Page 607. December 1903. 13 illustrations.

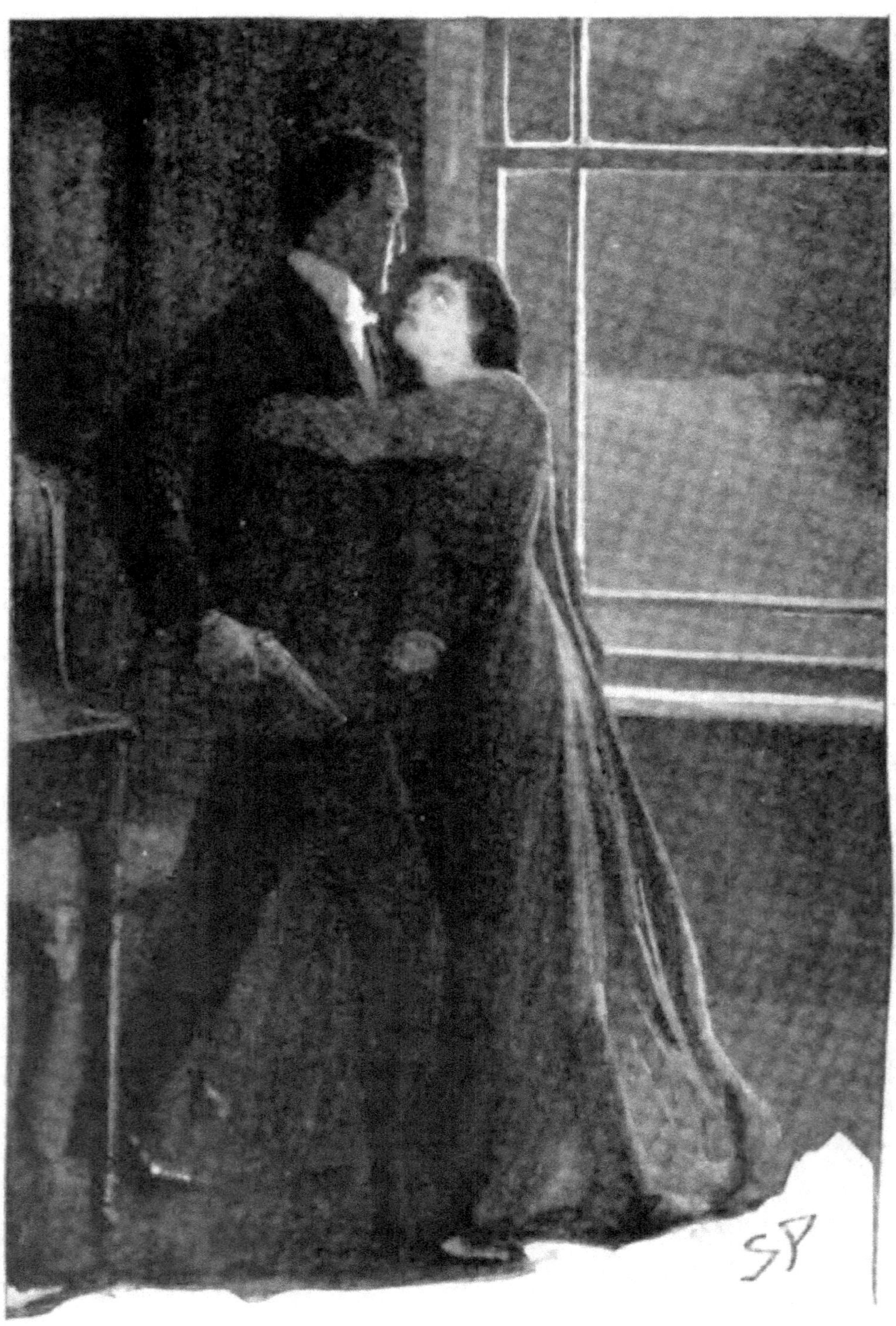

Image 9/13. "My wife threw her arms round me."
Ref. SH-SP278

Sidney Paget – The Adventure of the Dancing Men. The Strand Magazine Page 609. December 1903. 13 illustrations.

Image 10/13. "I suppose that you are the detectives from London?' said he."
Ref. SH-SP279

Sidney Paget – The Adventure of the Dancing Men. The Strand Magazine Page 609. December 1903. 13 illustrations.

Image 11/13. Page 609 "They both remembered that they were conscious of the smell of powder."
Ref. SH-SP280

Sidney Paget – The Adventure of the Dancing Men. The Strand Magazine Page 612. December 1903. 13 illustrations.

Image 12/13. "He bent forward and picked up a little brazen cylinder."
Ref. SH-SP281

Sidney Paget – The Adventure of the Dancing Men. The Strand Magazine Page 615. December 1903. 13 illustrations.

Image 13/13. “He buried his face in his manacled hands.”
Ref. SH-SP282

Sidney Paget – The Adventure of the Solitary Cyclist. The Strand Magazine Page 2. January 1904. 7 illustrations.

Image 1/7. "He spun round with a scream and fell upon his back."
Ref. SH-SP283

(See page 11.)

Sidney Paget – The Adventure of the Solitary Cyclist. The Strand Magazine Page 4. January 1904. 7 illustrations.

Image 2/7. "My friend took the lady's ungloved hand and examined it."
Ref. SH-SP284

Sidney Paget – The Adventure of the Solitary Cyclist. The Strand Magazine Page 6. January 1904. 7 illustrations.

Image 3/7. “I slowed down my machine.”
Ref. SH-SP285

Sidney Paget – The Adventure of the Solitary Cyclist. The Strand Magazine Page 9. January 1904. 7 illustrations.

Image 4/7. “A straight left against a slogging ruffian.”
Ref. SH-SP286

Sidney Paget – The Adventure of the Solitary Cyclist. The Strand Magazine Page 10. January 1904. 7 illustrations.

Image 5/7. " 'Too late, Watson: too late!' cried Holmes."
Ref. SH-SP287

Sidney Paget – The Adventure of the Solitary Cyclist. The Strand Magazine Page 12. January 1904. 7 illustrations.

Image 6/7. "As we approached, the lady staggered against the trunk of the tree."
Ref. SH-SP288

Sidney Paget – The Adventure of the Solitary Cyclist. The Strand Magazine Page 14. January 1904. 7 illustrations.

Image 7/7. "Holmes rose and tossed the end of his cigarette into the grate."
Ref. SH-SP289

Sidney Paget – The Adventure of the Priory School. The Strand Magazine Page 122. February 1904. 10 illustrations.

Image 1/10. "I heard him chuckle as the light fell upon a patched Dunlop tyre."
Ref. SH-SP290

(See page 135.)

Sidney Paget – The Adventure of the Priory School. The Strand Magazine Page 124. February 1904. 10 illustrations.

Image 2/10. "The heavy white face was seamed with lines of trouble."
Ref. SH-SP291

Sidney Paget – The Adventure of the Priory School. The Strand Magazine Page 126. February 1904. 10 illustrations.

Image 3/10. "What is the theory in your mind?"
Ref. SH-SP292

Sidney Paget – The Adventure of the Priory School. The Strand Magazine Page 128. February 1904. 10 illustrations.

Image 4/10. "Beside him stood a very young man."
Ref. SH-SP293

Sidney Paget – The Adventure of the Priory School. The Strand Magazine Page 130. February 1904. 10 illustrations.

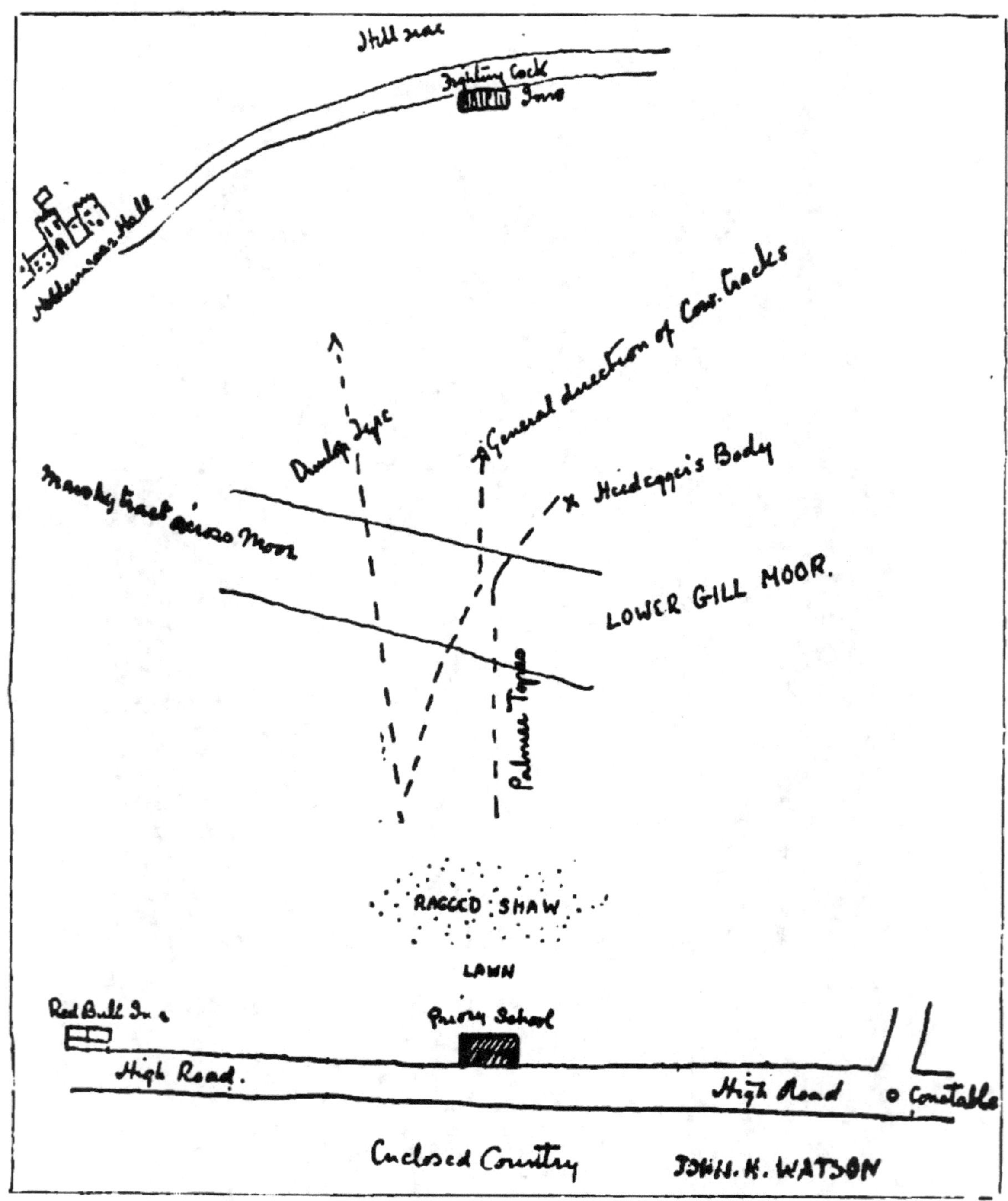

Image 5/10. "Sketch map showing the locality."

Sidney Paget – The Adventure of the Priory School. The Strand Magazine Page 131. February 1904. 10 illustrations.

Image 6/10. "An impression like a fine bundle of telegraph wires ran down the centre of it."
Ref. SH-SP294

Sidney Paget – The Adventure of the Priory School. The Strand Magazine Page 132. February 1904. 10 illustrations.

Image 7/10. "There lay the unfortunate rider."
Ref. SH-SP295

Sidney Paget – The Adventure of the Priory School. The Strand Magazine Page 134. February 1904. 10 illustrations.

Image 8/10. “With difficulty he limped up to the door.”
Ref. SH-SP296

Sidney Paget – The Adventure of the Priory School. The Strand Magazine Page 136. February 1904. 10 illustrations.

Image 9/10. “The man flew past us on the road.”
Ref. SH-SP297

Sidney Paget – The Adventure of the Priory School. The Strand Magazine Page 138. February 1904. 10 illustrations.

Image 10/10. "The murderer has escaped."
Ref. SH-SP298

Sidney Paget – The Adventure of Black Peter. The Strand Magazine Page 242. March 1904. 7 illustrations.

Image 1/7. "He sank down upon the sea chest, and looked helplessly from one of us to the other."
Ref. SH-SP299

(See page 250.)

Sidney Paget – The Adventure of Black Peter. The Strand Magazine Page 244. March 1904. 7 illustrations.

Image 2/7. " 'Good gracious, Holmes!' I cried, 'You don't mean to say that you have been walking about London with that thing?' "
Ref. SH-SP300

Sidney Paget – The Adventure of Black Peter. The Strand Magazine Page 247. March 1904. 7 illustrations.

Image 3/7. "Holmes examined it in his minute way."
Ref. SH-SP301

Sidney Paget – The Adventure of Black Peter. The Strand Magazine Page 248. March 1904. 7 illustrations.

Image 4/7. " 'Someone has been tampering with it' he said."
Ref. SH-SP302

Sidney Paget – The Adventure of Black Peter. The Strand Magazine Page 250. March 1904. 7 illustrations.

Image 5/7. "He rapidly turned over the leaves of this volume."
Ref. SH-SP303

Sidney Paget – The Adventure of Black Peter. The Strand Magazine Page 253. March 1904. 7 illustrations.

Image 6/7. " 'Shall I sign here?' he asked."
Ref. SH-SP304

Sidney Paget – The Adventure of Black Peter. The Strand Magazine Page 254. March 1904. 7 illustrations.

Image 7/7. “We sat down and we drank and we yarned about old times.”
Ref. SH-SP305

Sidney Paget – The Adventure of Charles Augustus Milverton. The Strand Magazine Page 374. April 1904. 6 illustrations.

Image 1/6. “Charles Augustus Milverton.”
Ref. SH-SP306

Sidney Paget – The Adventure of Charles Augustus Milverton. The Strand Magazine Page 376. April 1904. 6 illustrations.

Image 2/6. "Exhibiting the butt of a large revolver, which projected from the inside pocket."
Ref. SH-SP307

Sidney Paget – The Adventure of Charles Augustus Milverton. The Strand Magazine Page 379. April 1904. 6 illustrations.

Image 3/6. "He stood with slanting head listening intently."
Ref. SH-SP308

Sidney Paget – The Adventure of Charles Augustus Milverton. The Strand Magazine Page 380. April 1904. 6 illustrations.

Image 4/6. “You couldn’t come any other time -eh?”
Ref. SH-SP309

Sidney Paget – The Adventure of Charles Augustus Milverton. The Strand Magazine Page 382. April 1904. 6 illustrations.

Image 5/6. "Then he staggered to his feet and received another shot."
Ref. SH-SP310

Sidney Paget – The Adventure of Charles Augustus Milverton. The Strand Magazine Page 383. April 1904. 6 illustrations.

Image 6/6. "Following his gaze I saw the picture of a regal and stately lady in a court dress."
Ref. SH-SP311

Sidney Paget – The Adventure of the Six Napoleons. The Strand Magazine Page 482. May 1904. 7 illustrations.

Image 1/7. "With the bound of a tiger Holmes was on his back."
Ref. SH-SP312

(See page 492.)

Sidney Paget – The Adventure of the Six Napoleons. The Strand Magazine Page 484. May 1904. 7 illustrations.

Image 2/7. "Lestrade took out his official note-book."
Ref. SH-SP313

Sidney Paget – The Adventure of the Six Napoleons. The Strand Magazine Page 486. May 1904. 7 illustrations.

Image 3/7. "He was introduced to us as the owner of the house – Mr. Horace Harker."
Ref. SH-SP314

Sidney Paget – The Adventure of the Six Napoleons. The Strand Magazine Page 488. May 1904. 7 illustrations.

Image 4/7. “Holmes pointed to the street lamp above our heads.”
Ref. SH-SP315

Sidney Paget – The Adventure of the Six Napoleons. The Strand Magazine Page 490. May 1904. 7 illustrations.

Image 5/7. " 'Ah, the rascal!' he cried."
Ref. SH-SP316

Sidney Paget – The Adventure of the Six Napoleons. The Strand Magazine Page 492. May 1904. 7 illustrations.

Image 6/7. “The door opened, and the owner of the house presented himself.”
Ref. SH-SP317

Sidney Paget – The Adventure of the Six Napoleons. The Strand Magazine Page 494. May 1904. 7 illustrations.

Image 7/7. “I brought the bust up with me, as you asked me to do.”
Ref. SH-SP318

Sidney Paget – The Adventure of the Three Students. The Strand Magazine Page 602. June 1904. 7 illustrations.

Image 1/7. " 'Come, come,' said Holmes kindly. 'It is human to err.' "
Ref. SH-SP319

Sidney Paget – The Adventure of the Three Students. The Strand Magazine Page 604. June 1904. 7 illustrations.

Image 2/7. "How could you possibly know that!"
Ref. SH-SP320

Sidney Paget – The Adventure of the Three Students. The Strand Magazine Page 606. June 1904. 7 illustrations.

Image 3/7. "With his neck craned, he looked into the room."
Ref. SH-SP321

Sidney Paget – The Adventure of the Three Students. The Strand Magazine Page 608. June 1904. 7 illustrations.

Image 4/7. "How came you to leave the key in the door?."
Ref. SH-SP322

Sidney Paget – The Adventure of the Three Students. The Strand Magazine Page 609. June 1904. 7 illustrations.

Image 5/7. “He insisted on drawing it in his note-book.”
Ref. SH-SP323

Sidney Paget – The Adventure of the Three Students. The Strand Magazine Page 611. June 1904. 7 illustrations.

Image 6/7. "An instant later the tutor returned, bringing with him the student."
Ref. SH-SP324

Sidney Paget – The Adventure of the Three Students. The Strand Magazine Page 613. June 1904. 7 illustrations.

Image 7/7. “Here it is, sir.”
Ref. SH-SP325

Sidney Paget – The Adventure of the Golden Pince-Nez. The Strand Magazine Page 2. July 1904. 9 illustrations.

Image 1/9. "Holmes had bounded across the room and had wrenched a small phial from her hand."
Ref. SH-SP326

(See page 16.)

Sidney Paget – The Adventure of the Golden Pince-Nez. The Strand Magazine Page 4. July 1904. 9 illustrations.

Image 2/9. "It was young Stanley Hopkins, a promising detective."
Ref. SH-SP327

Sidney Paget – The Adventure of the Golden Pince-Nez. The Strand Magazine Page 6. July 1904. 9 illustrations.

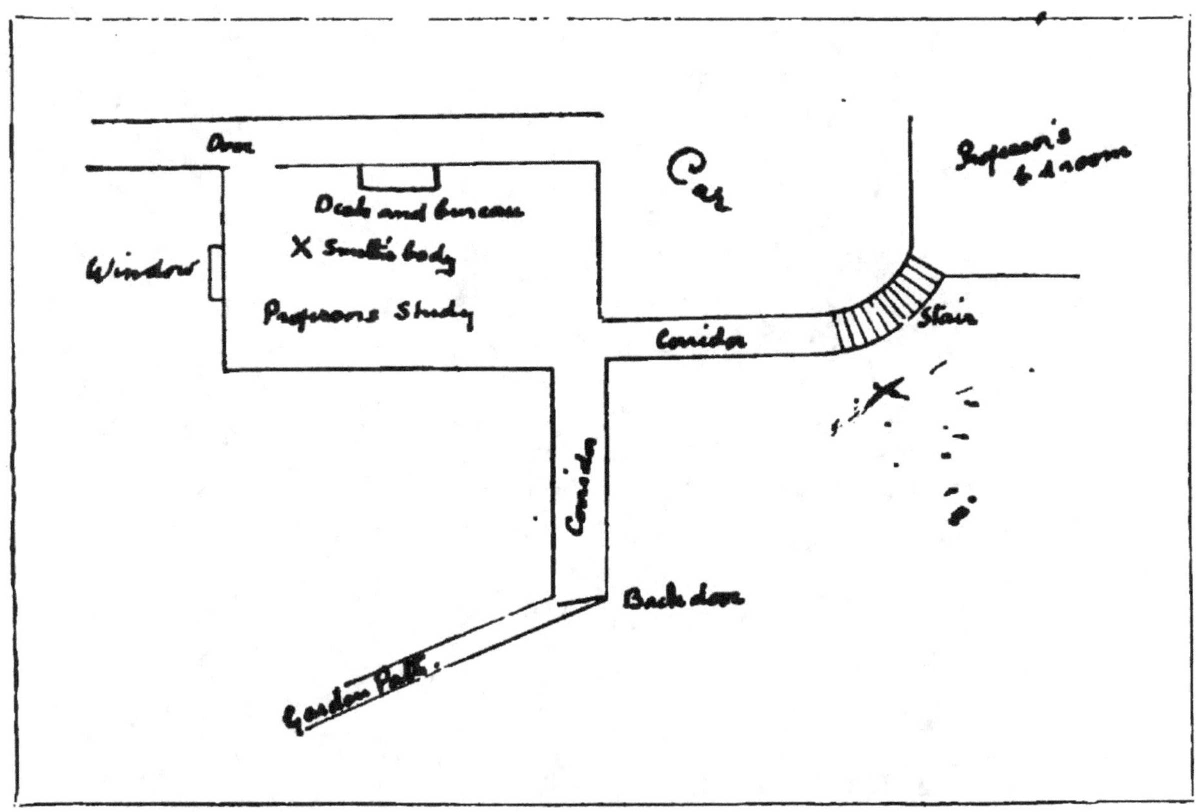

Image 3/9. “Map of Yoxley Old Place .”

Sidney Paget – The Adventure of the Golden Pince-Nez. The Strand Magazine Page 7. July 1904. 9 illustrations.

Image 4/9. "The body was found near the bureau, and just to the left of it, as marked upon that chart."
Ref. SH-SP328

Sidney Paget – The Adventure of the Golden Pince-Nez. The Strand Magazine Page 8. July 1904. 9 illustrations.

Image 5/9. "He endeavour to read through them."
Ref. SH-SP329

Sidney Paget – The Adventure of the Golden Pince-Nez. The Strand Magazine Page 10. July 1904. 9 illustrations.

Image 6/9. “Did you dust this bureau yesterday morning?”
Ref. SH-SP330

Sidney Paget – The Adventure of the Golden Pince-Nez. The Strand Magazine Page 12. July 1904. 9 illustrations.

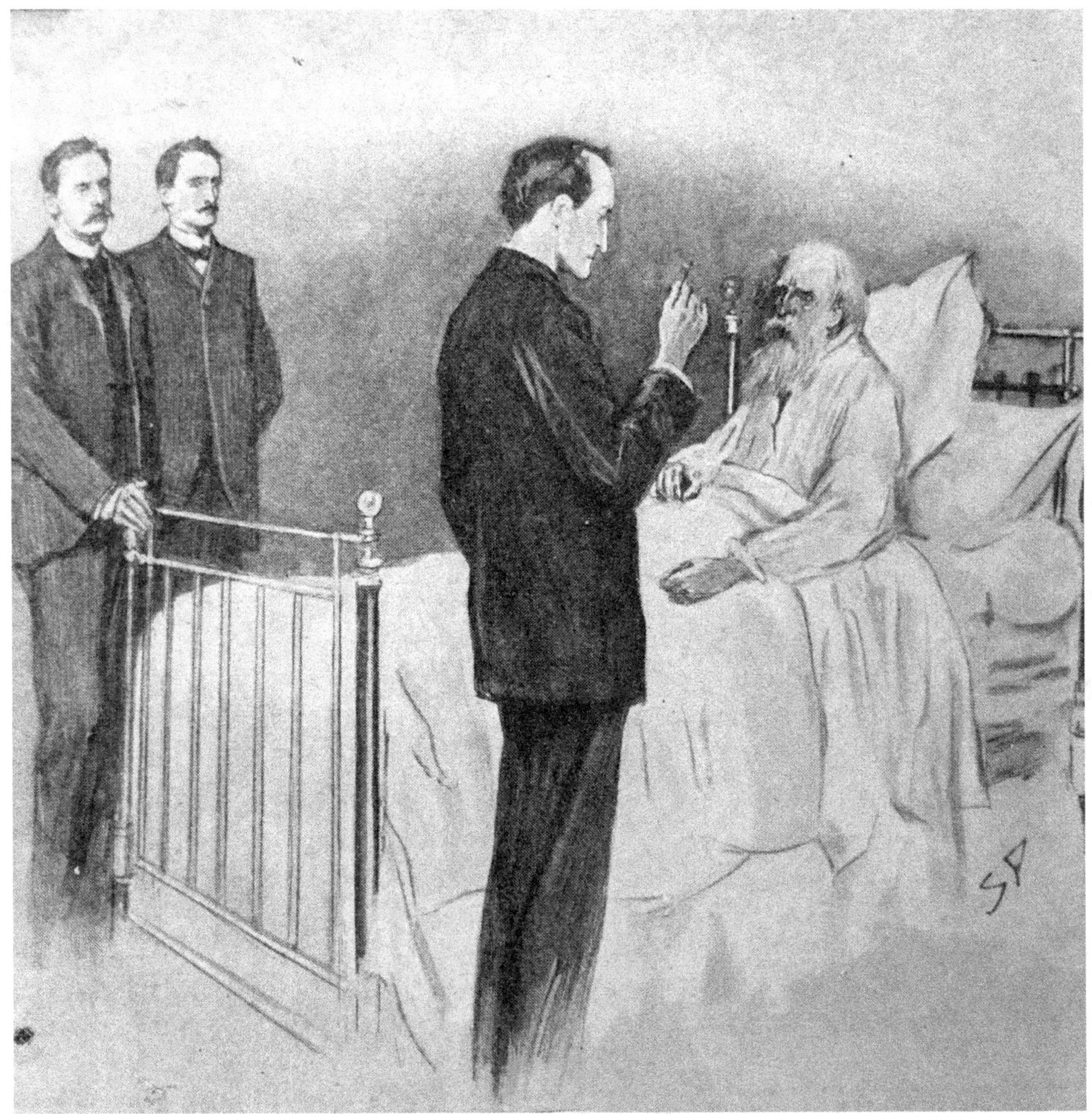

Image 7/9. "Holmes picked up the key and looked at it for an instant."
Ref. SH-SP331

Sidney Paget – The Adventure of the Golden Pince-Nez. The Strand Magazine Page 14. July 1904. 9 illustrations.

Image 8/9. "A woman rushed out into the room."
Ref. SH-SP332

Sidney Paget – The Adventure of the Golden Pince-Nez. The Strand Magazine Page 15. July 1904. 9 illustrations.

Image 9/9. " 'I am in your hands, Anna,' said he.
Ref. SH-SP333

Sidney Paget – The Adventure of the Missing Three-Quarter. The Strand Magazine Page 122. August 1904. 9 illustrations.

Image 1/9. "The carriage rattled past."
Ref. SH-SP334

(See page 134.)

Sidney Paget – The Adventure of the Missing Three-Quarter. The Strand Magazine Page 124. August 1904. 9 illustrations.

Image 2/9. " 'Why, Mr. Holmes, I thought you knew things,' said he."
Ref. SH-SP335

Sidney Paget – The Adventure of the Missing Three-Quarter. The Strand Magazine Page 126. August 1904. 9 illustrations.

Image 3/9. "Did you take any messages to Mr. Staunton?"
Ref. SH-SP336

Sidney Paget – The Adventure of the Missing Three-Quarter. The Strand Magazine Page 127. August 1904. 9 illustrations.

Image 4/9. “Strip of blotting paper.”

Sidney Paget – The Adventure of the Missing Three-Quarter. The Strand Magazine Page 127. August 1904

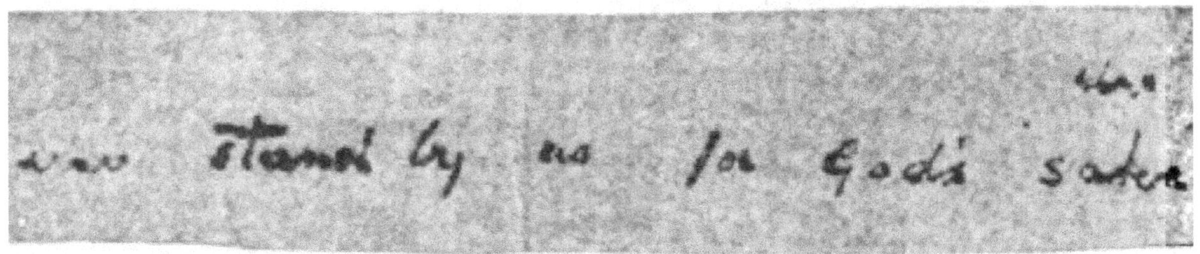

Image 5/9. “and looking though the blotting paper, Holmes read the message.”

Sidney Paget – The Adventure of the Missing Three-Quarter. The Strand Magazine Page 128. August 1904. 9 illustrations.

Image 6/9. " 'One moment, one moment!' cried a querulous voice."
Ref. SH-SP337

Sidney Paget – The Adventure of the Missing Three-Quarter. The Strand Magazine Page 130. August 1904. 9 illustrations.

Image 7/9. "He looked up with no very pleased expression on his dour features."
Ref. SH-SP338

Sidney Paget – The Adventure of the Missing Three-Quarter. The Strand Magazine Page 133. August 1904. 9 illustrations.

Image 8/9. “We were clear of the town and hastening down a country road.”
Ref. SH-SP339

Sidney Paget – The Adventure of the Missing Three-Quarter. The Strand Magazine Page 135. August 1904. 9 illustrations.

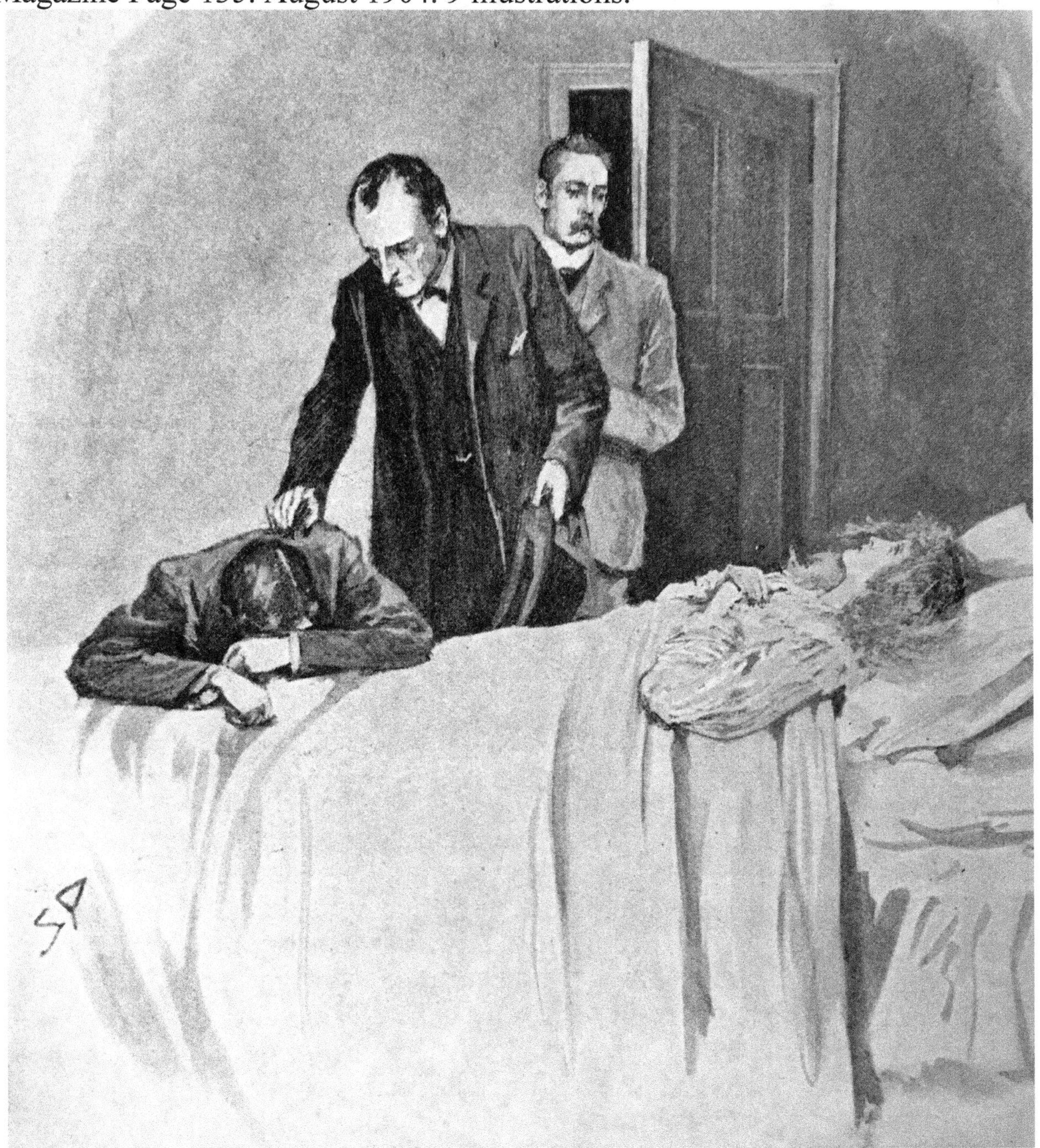

Image 9/9. He never looked up until Holmes' hand was on his shoulder.
Ref. SH-SP340

Sidney Paget – The Adventure of the Abbey Grange. The Strand Magazine Page 242. September 1904. 8 illustrations.

Image 1/8. "It was the body of a tall, well-made man, about forty years of age."

Ref. SH-SP341

(See page 247.)

Sidney Paget – The Adventure of the Abbey Grange. The Strand Magazine Page 243. September 1904. 8 illustrations.

Image 2/8. "'Come, Watson, come!' he cried. 'The game is afoot.'"
Ref. SH-SP342

Sidney Paget – The Adventure of the Abbey Grange. The Strand Magazine Page 245. September 1904. 8 illustrations.

Image 3/8. “I am the wife of Sir Eustace Brackenstall.”
Ref. SH-SP343

Sidney Paget – The Adventure of the Abbey Grange. The Strand Magazine Page 247. September 1904. 8 illustrations.

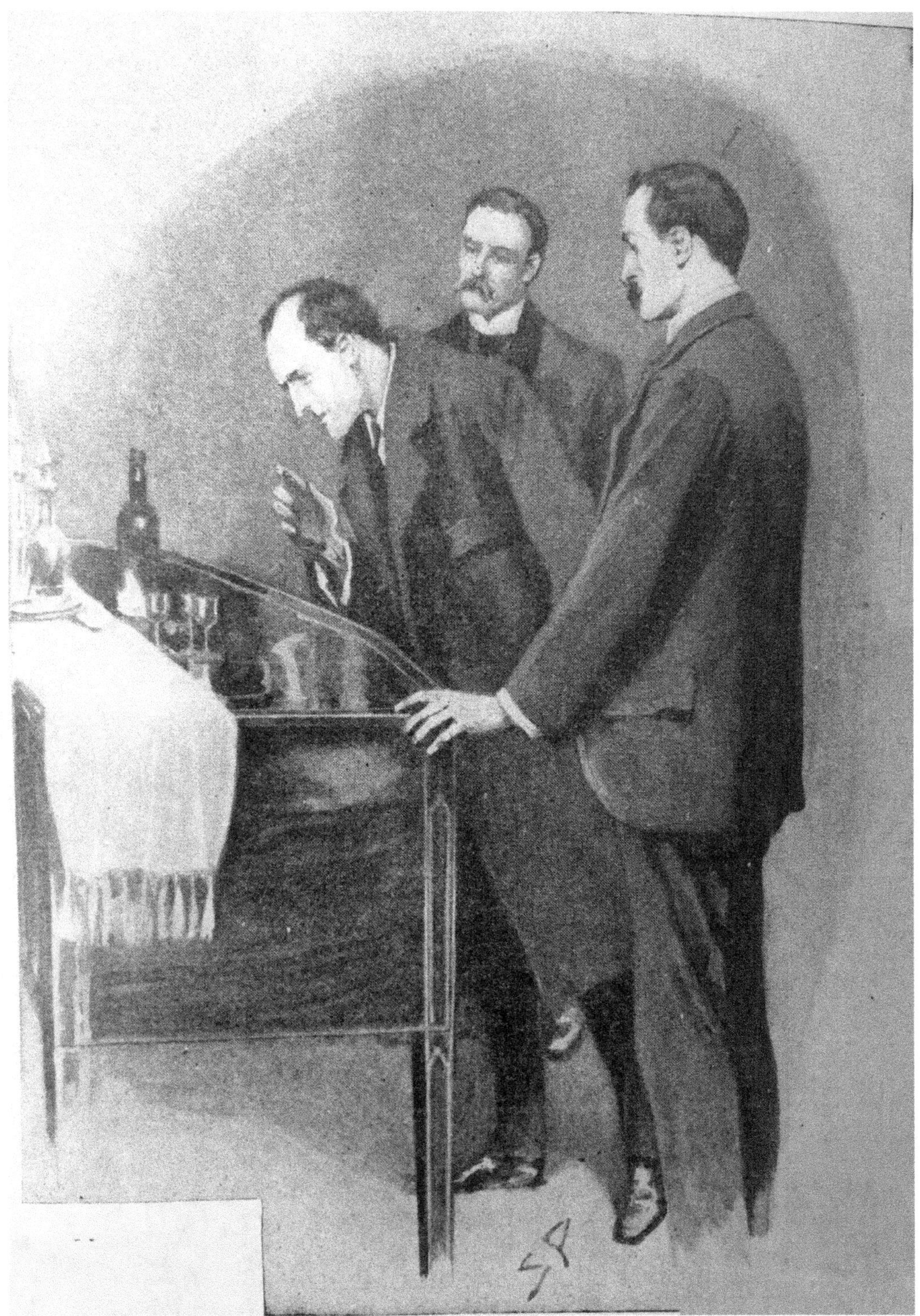

Image 4/8. “Halloa, halloa, what is this?”
Ref. SH-SP344

Sidney Paget – The Adventure of the Abbey Grange. The Strand Magazine Page 249. September 1904. 8 illustrations.

Image 5/8. "I could see by Holmes's face that he was much puzzled."
Ref. SH-SP345

Sidney Paget – The Adventure of the Abbey Grange. The Strand Magazine Page 251. September 1904. 8 illustrations.

Image 6/8. "Look at that mark on the seat of the oaken chair!"
Ref. SH-SP346

Sidney Paget – The Adventure of the Abbey Grange. The Strand Magazine Page 253. September 1904. 8 illustrations.

Image 7/8. "Holmes gazed at it and then passed on."
Ref. SH-SP347

Sidney Paget – The Adventure of the Abbey Grange. The Strand Magazine Page 255. September 1904. 8 illustrations.

Image 8/8. “The door was opened to admit as fine a specimen of manhood as ever passed through it.”
Ref. SH-SP348

Sidney Paget – The Adventure of the Second Stain. The Strand Magazine Page 602. October 1904. 8 illustrations.

Image 1/8. "It hinged back like the lid of a box."
Ref. SH-SP349

(See page 613.)

Sidney Paget – The Adventure of the Second Stain. The Strand Magazine Page 604. October 1904. 8 illustrations.

Image 2/8. “They sat side by side.”
Ref. SH-SP350

Sidney Paget – The Adventure of the Second Stain. The Strand Magazine Page 606. October 1904. 8 illustrations.

Image 3/8. “The premier sprang to his feet.”
Ref. SH-SP351

Sidney Paget – The Adventure of the Second Stain. The Strand Magazine Page 608. October 1904. 8 illustrations.

Image 4/8. "My dear Watson, the two events are connected – must be connected."
Ref. SH-SP352

Sidney Paget – The Adventure of the Second Stain. The Strand Magazine Page 610. October 1904. 8 illustrations.

Image 5/8. "She looked back at us from the door."
Ref. SH-SP353

Sidney Paget – The Adventure of the Second Stain. The Strand Magazine Page 612. October 1904. 8 illustrations.

Image 6/8. "He took the corner of the carpet in his hand."
Ref. SH-SP354

Sidney Paget – The Adventure of the Second Stain. The Strand Magazine Page 614. October 1904. 8 illustrations.

Image 7/8. “You insult me, Mr. Holmes.”
Ref. SH-SP355

Sidney Paget – The Adventure of the Second Stain. The Strand Magazine Page 617. October 1904. 8 illustrations.

Image 8/8. "The premier snatched the blue envelope from his hand."
Ref. SH-SP356

Paget, Walter Stanley

Born 26th January 1862 in London, Died 29th January 1935 in Fockbury, Worcestershire.
Signed his work Wal Paget.
Youngest of the three Paget brothers. He didn't get the big Sherlock Holmes Gig with the Strand Magazine, but did 4 illustrates for the Holmes story 'The Dying Detective'.

Sidney's Younger brother Walter Paget

Sidney's Illustration of Holmes, taken from 'The Naval Treaty' story

Walter Paget – The Adventure of the Dying Detective. The Strand Magazine Page 602. December 1913. 4 illustrations.

Image 1/4. "Put it down! Down, this instant, Watson – this instant, I say!"
Ref. SH-WP1

(See page 608.)

Walter Paget – The Adventure of the Dying Detective. The Strand Magazine Page 607. December 1913. 4 illustrations.

Image 2/4. "I heard the sharp snap of a twisted key."
Ref. SH-WP2

Walter Paget – The Adventure of the Dying Detective. The Strand Magazine Page 611. December 1913. 4 illustrations.

Image 3/4. " 'What's this?' he cried, in a high, screaming voice. 'What is the meaning of this intrusion?' "
Ref. SH-WP3

Walter Paget – The Adventure of the Dying Detective. The Strand Magazine Page 613. December 1913. 4 illustrations.

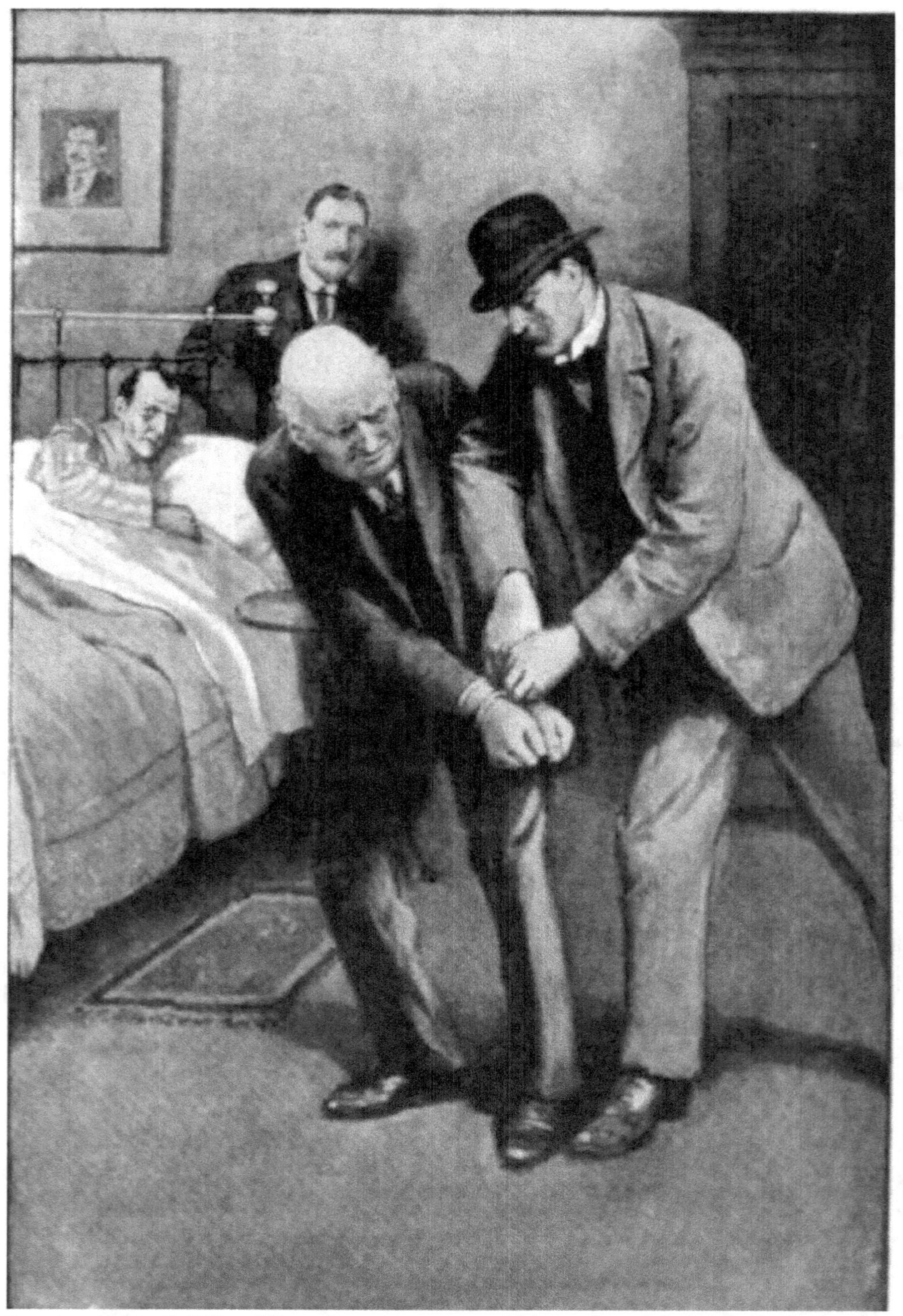

Image 4/4. " 'You'll only get yourself hurt,' said the inspector".
Ref. SH-WP

www.ingramcontent.com/pod-product-compliance
Lightning Source LLC
Chambersburg PA
CBHW081134300726
48982CB00005B/961
* 9 7 8 1 7 8 7 0 5 8 2 5 5 *